DOM
&
BECCA

WILLOW WINTERS
WALL STREET JOURNAL & USA TODAY BESTSELLING AUTHOR

From USA Today bestselling author Willow Winters comes a HOT mafia, standalone romance.

I'm not always proud of the man I am, but when you grow up in a crime family, there aren't a lot of options.

I do what I have to do, and more than often, I crave it. The power, the women, the money. All of it comes easy to me.

Until Becca walked into my office. Everything about her was tempting. Her beautiful eyes that pierced into me, her body that was made for sin.

She came to pay off a debt, but I wanted more. So I did what I've always done, I took what I wanted.

She's a good girl who never should have walked through that door. I never should have touched her, but now that I have, I can't stop. I'll push her boundaries, she'll cave to temptation. We'll both forget about the danger.

And that's a mistake I can't afford...

DIRTY DOM

PROLOGUE

Dom

    I crack my knuckles and stretch my arms above my head while looking out over the football stadium from my suite. I fucking love that this is my office. But then again, when you do what I do, your "office" can be anywhere. I snatch my scotch from the bar and tell Johnny to grab our lunch. Taking a seat on the sectional, I pull out my phone to look at my schedule. My first drop-off should be here soon.

Becca

    I'm so fucking nervous. I click my phone on and see I have fifteen minutes to find the bookie's suite. I clutch my purse tighter, holding the Coach Hobo closer to my side. I've got twelve thousand in cash under a scarf, and the idea I'm going to be mugged and then killed by the bookie is making my blood rush with adrenaline and anxiety. I can't believe Rick would put me in this position. Shit. I'm such a bitch. I swallow the lump in my throat and square my shoulders to keep the tears pricking the back of my eyes from surfacing. Now is not the time to think about Rick. And it's not like he asked me to do this. His problems keep coming after me, and I want to cover my bases.

The knock at the door seems hesitant, and that makes a deep, rough chuckle rumble in my hard chest. Whoever's behind the door is scared, and I live for that fear. They're right to be scared. I didn't get where I am today by being kind and understanding. Fuck that. I'm a ruthless prick, and I know it. Doubt fills my chest for a fraction of a second, but I shut that shit down ASAP. I'm a tough fucker, and I'm not going to let some pussy emotions make me weak. Some days I wish I didn't have to be such a cruel asshole. I don't like fucking guys up, breaking their legs and hands or whatever body part they pick – if I let them choose. But they know what they're signing up for when they do business with me. Damn shame they don't have a doctorate degree in Statistics from Stanford, like me. A devilish grin pulls at my lips. If you're gonna be making bets with me, you better be ready to pay up.

I wipe the cold sweat from my hands and onto my dress, ball up my small fist even tighter and knock on the door a little harder. I wonder if the people walking by know why I'm here. I swallow thickly, feeling like a dirty criminal. My eyes dart to an older woman with kind eyes and grey-speckled hair pushing a caterer's cart past me. I'm sure she knows. I'm sure everyone who looks at me knows I'm up to no good.

My eyes glance from left to right as I wait impatiently. Sarah's waiting outside, and I have to pick up my son from soccer practice soon. I lick my lower lip as the nerves start to creep up again. I'll just pretend this isn't real. Just hand them the money and walk away. Back to real life. Back to my assistant, and move on with my normal, nonthreatening, everyday life.

I take my time getting to the door. No matter how much money they owe me, or how much they've won, they need to know I do everything whenever the fuck I please. If they have to wait, they have to wait. But I sure as shit don't wait for them. I open the door and my cold, hard heart pumps with hot blood and desire.

A petite woman in fuck-me pink heels and a grey dress that clings to her curves and ends just above her knees is staring back at me with wide, frightened hazel eyes. Her breasts rise and fall, peeking out of the modest neckline. Her black cardigan is covering up too much of her chest, and I narrowly resist the urge to push it off her shoulders. My eyes travel along her body in obvious appreciation before stopping at her purse. She's clinging to it like it's her lifeline. A tic in my jaw starts to twitch. What's a woman like her doing

making bets with a guy like me? Johnny handles most of that shit now. We aren't supposed to take bets from women. I don't like it. I'm definitely going to have to ask him about her.

The door opens, and I nervously peek up through my thick, dark lashes at the gorgeous man looking down at me. The lines around his eyes mean he's every bit the man he looks, but his devilish white-toothed grin gives him a boyish charm meant to fool women like me. He's fucking hot in a black three-piece suit that's obviously been tailored to fit his large chiseled frame perfectly. With that crisp white button-down shirt and simple black tie you'd think he was a young CEO, but his muscular body, piercing blue eyes and messy dark hair that's long enough to grab, make him a sex god. Lust and power radiate from his broad chest as his eyes travel down my body. He looks like a man who knows how to destroy you.

A wave of desire shoots through me when my eyes meet his heated stare. My breathing hitches, and I swallow down the distress I'm feeling at my treacherous body. I'll just give him the money Rick owed him and get the fuck out of here. At the reminder of why I'm standing in his doorway, I push my purse toward him.

I grin at her obvious nervousness and cock a brow as I say, "Purses aren't my style, doll." Pulling the door open wider, I step aside just enough for her to get through. Her soft body gently brushes against mine as she walks through the small opening I gave her. The subtle touch sends a throbbing need

to my dick and I feel it harden, pushing against my zipper. She hustles a little quicker when I lean closer to her. Her hips sway, and I stifle a groan when I see that dress clinging to her lush ass. Fuck, I want that ass. I never mix business with pleasure, but there's an exception to every rule. Something about her just pulls me in. Something about the way she's carrying herself. It's like she needs me, or maybe I need her. My dick jumps as she turns around to fully face me. Fuck, at least one part of me desperately wants her attention.

His body touching mine makes every nerve ending in my core ignite; I nervously squeeze the strap of my purse. I just want to get the hell out of here, but my stupid heart is longing for comfort. My trembling body is aching with need. What the hell is wrong with me? It's only been three days; I should have more respect for Rick than this. I will the tears to go away. I just want to be held. But I know better. This man staring back at me isn't a man who will hold me and console me. I take in a gasp of air and turn around to face the man my husband owed money to while digging in my purse to gather the bundles of cash.

"Is it all there?" I have no fucking clue who she is, or what she's supposed to be giving me. Johnny has the list, but he's not back yet with our lunch. It's a rarity that I even have to speak during drops. I just like to watch. And when it comes to people not paying up, it's best if I'm here for that.

"I'm sorry it's late." His rough fingers brush mine as I

hold out the thick stacks of hundreds. His touch sends a shot of lust to my heated core and I close my eyes, denying the desperate need burning inside me. It would feel so good to let him take me the way a man should. I haven't been touched in months. I haven't felt desire in nearly a year, and I know for a fact I've never felt such a strong pull to a man before, never wanted to give myself to someone like I do him.

"What about the interest?" Her eyes widen with fear, and her breath stalls as her plump lips part. If it's late, then she should know to pay that extra five percent per day. Compounded. Johnny should've told her all that shit. But judging by her silence and that scared look on her face, she doesn't have a clue. A grin pulls at my lips, but I stifle it. I want her to think I'm mad. I want her to feel like she owes me. I don't want her money though. She can pay me in a way I've never been paid before. I don't accept ass as payment, but for her, fuck yeah I'll take it.

The man on the phone said not to worry about being late. He said he was sorry for my loss, and that he understood. I feel my breath coming up short as a lump grows in my throat. Fuck! What the hell am I going to do? Fucking Rick, leaving me with this shit to deal with. I wish I could just fucking hide as these damn tears start pricking my eyes. My hands start to shake as I realize I'm trapped in the bookie's suite and I owe him more money that I don't have.

"Aw, doll. Don't cry. We can work something out." Her bottom lip's trembling, and her gorgeous hazel eyes are brimming with tears. I feel like a fucking asshole for taking advantage of the situation. But then again, what the fuck did she expect? First, she made a bet with a bookie – not fucking smart on her part. Then she's late with handing over the dough. She had to know there'd be consequences. She parts her lips to respond, but she's too shaken up. My heart clenches looking at her small frame quaking with worry.

I'll make it good for her. She looks like a girl I could keep. My brow furrows as I reach out to brush her cheek with my hand. I'm not sure where that thought came from, but the more I think about it, the more I like it. She closes her eyes and leans into my touch as I wipe away the tears trailing down her sun-kissed skin. As I reach her lips, I part them with my thumb.

I hate the bastard tears that've escaped. I feel too raw and vulnerable. I can't help but love the warmth of his skin. How long has it been since someone's touched me with kindness and looked at me with desire? I *need* this. I need to be held, if only for a little while. His thumb brushes my bottom lip, and I instantly part them for him. He can hold me for a moment. I can pretend it's more. I can pretend he really wants me. I can pretend he loves me.

Fuck, she's so damn perfect. She's leaning into me like

she really wants me. Like she needs me. She radiates sweet innocence, but there's something more about her, something I can't quite put my finger on. A sting of loneliness pulses through me. I was playing with the thought of having her on her knees in exchange for payment. But I want more. I want her to fucking love what I do to her. I'll make her want me when it's over. A coldness sweeps through me. Women always act like they want me after, but it's the money they want, not me. A sad smirk plays at my lips as she licks my thumb and massages the underside with her hot tongue. Fuck, I'll take it. If she only wants me for my money, I'll take it. I feel a burning need to keep her.

My brows creases with anger at my thoughts. My fucking heart is turning me into a little bitch. "Strip. Now." My words come out hard, making her take a hesitant step back as I pull my thumb from her lips. I instantly regret being the fucking asshole I am. But I can't take it back. I turn my back to her, to lock the door. I slip the gun out from under my belt and easily hide it from her sight to set it down on the table by the door. God knows what she'd think if she got a look at it.

My body flinches as the hard sound of the door locking echoes through the room. He moves with power and confidence, his gaze like one of a predator. I swallow my pride and slip off my cardigan. I don't need pride and self-respect right now; I need a man to desire me. The thought and his hungry eyes on me have me peeling off my dress without hesitation. I don't care if this is a payment or if he's just using the interest as an excuse to fuck me; I want this. Or at least I want him.

As I reach behind my back to unhook my bra, he reaches for me, wrapping his strong arms around my body and molding his hard chest to mine. His lips crush against mine, and I part them for his hot tongue to taste me. He kisses me with passion and need. His hard dick pushes into my stomach. The feeling makes my pussy heat and clench. Yes. The tears stop, but my chest is still in agony. *Make it go away, please. Take my pain away.*

She fucking needs me; I can feel it. And I sure as fuck need her. I don't even hesitate to unleash my rigid cock from my pants. I rip her skimpy lace panties from her body, easily shredding them and tossing them to the floor. I squeeze her lush ass in my hands, pulling her body to mine. I slam her against the wall, keeping my lips to hers the entire time. My chest pounds as hot blood pumps through me. I need to be inside her now. I line my dick up with her hot entrance, rubbing my head between her slick pussy lips.

Fuck, she wants me just as much I want her. I slam inside of her, all the way to the hilt. She breaks our kiss to lean her head back, banging it against the wall and screaming out with pleasure as I fuck her tight pussy recklessly. My right hand roams her body while my left keeps her pinned to the wall.

Her arousal leaks from her hot pussy and down to my thighs.

My legs wrap tightly around him as he ruts into me with a primitive need. My body knows I need his touch, but my heart needs his lips and it clenches as he gives them to me. He frantically kisses me as he pounds into me with desperation. The position he has me in ensures he pushes against my throbbing clit with each thrust. I feel my body building toward my release, every nerve ending on high alert.

His lips trail down my neck to my shoulder and collarbone, leaving small bites and open-mouth kisses in his wake. He licks the dip in my throat before trailing his hot tongue back up my neck. I moan my pleasure into the cold air above us. My heart stills, and my body trembles as a numbness and heat attack my body at once. "Yes!" I scream out as my pussy pulses around his thick cock. My body convulses against his as pleasure races through my heavy limbs. I feel waves of hot cum soak my aching pussy. My eyes widen as the aftershocks settle. What the fuck did I just do? I need to get out of here.

She's pushing against me like she can't wait to leave, and that makes my damn heart drop in my chest. Fine. It's fine. It's not like this was anything more than a payment. I say that over and over while I turn my back on her to grab my pants. I walk across the suite to grab a tissue from the desk for her to clean up with, but when I face her, she's already dressed. My blood runs cold with her dismissal of me and

what we just shared. It wasn't just some random fuck. There was something there. I've never felt like that before. I never felt THAT before. Whatever it is, I fucking want it. And I'm a man who gets what he wants. My conviction settles as I stride back to her. I'll have her again. I'll make sure it happens.

What the fuck have I done? I need to go. I have to go to my son. I want nothing more than for this man to hold me, but I know that's not going to happen. I'm so fucking stupid. I don't even know his name. These feelings in my fucked up chest aren't the same for him. This was just a payment. The thought makes my heart stop and my chest pain, but I brush it aside. I refuse to be any weaker in front of him. I need to be strong for just a moment longer. I try to fix my hair as best as I can without a mirror. I straighten my back and grab my purse as he walks back over to me.

Women like it when I'm an asshole. Don't know why and I don't care, but it always has them coming back to me. I definitely want to see this girl again; I fucking need to be inside her as often as I can. So after I walk her sweet ass to the door, I give her a cocky smirk and kiss her cheek.

He leans in and whispers against my ear, letting his hot breath tickle my neck, "Thanks for the payment, doll." With that he turns his back and shuts the door without giving me a second glance. That's the moment the lust-filled hope dies, and my heart cracks and crumbles in my hollow chest.

I count the money and start pacing. I need her info from Johnny. I need to know who this woman is. Whoever she is, she's going to end up being mine. Not five minutes after she's gone, Johnny comes back. "The first drop just left. She came with everything but the interest." I pocket her panties so he won't see them. "Twelve grand, right?"

"We didn't charge her interest; she didn't know about her husband's debt until yesterday."

"Since when is that how we do business?" I don't even try to keep my voice down. Blood starts pounding in my ears. "Why the fuck is she paying her husband's debt, anyway? He doesn't have the balls to come here himself? He sends his woman?!" The words jump from my lips before I have a moment to think.

I'm usually more controlled, more thoughtful. If this job has taught me anything, it's that silence is deadly, and being a hothead will get you killed. But I'm shaking with rage. Anger seeps out of my pores. Anger that she's married to a fucking coward and a bastard. But more than that, I'm fucking pissed that she's taken.

Johnny shakes his head in confusion and slows his movements as he takes in my temper. "No, it's not like that. He died last week, heart attack or something."

The moment Sarah sees me, the last bit of my hardened exterior cracks. I feel my lips tremble, and bite down to prevent the tears. "What did you do, Becca?" Sarah's pleading eyes makes me feel even shittier. She knows; she can tell. I'm sure I look like I just got fucked. My neck is pulsing from where he was biting me.

Her eyes want me to tell her she's wrong, and they're begging me to tell her she's mistaken, but I can't lie. I can feel his cum leaking out of me and running down my thigh. Evidence of my weakness, and my betrayal. The tears well up in my eyes and I can't stop a few from leaving angry, hot trails down my cheeks. All I can manage to reply is the barest of truths, "I slept with him."

"Don't cry, Becca. It's alright."

"Rick just died, and I slept with a stranger." I can't keep my own disgust out of my voice.

"It's not like you two were even together in the end anyway. You'd been separated for nearly two months." My breath comes in spasms as I rest my head on the door of my car. I loved my husband, but I can't remember the last time he held me, the last time we made love. A criminal who probably would've hurt me had I shown up empty-handed gave me more compassion and showed more desire for me than Rick had in years.

My breath catches in my throat. I took advantage of her in a moment of weakness, but I didn't fucking know how vulnerable she was. I slam my fist against the window. I

didn't fucking know! A sick, twisted churning in the pit of my stomach makes me want to heave. Fuck, I treated her like some random slut. She probably thinks I'm a fucking animal for doing that to her. Fuck! I knew she needed me. I fucking knew it.

I just needed to be held and feel like I was loved. This shattering feeling in my chest, jagged pieces of glass digging into my heart, tells me it wasn't worth it. It hurts too much. The worst part is that a very large part of me wants--no, *needs* to crawl back to him and beg him to hold me again. Just one more time.

I wish I hadn't let her go.

I wish I'd never had to meet with him.

I clench my teeth and close my eyes, wondering if I'll ever see her again.

I breathe deep and steady myself as I drive away, knowing I'll never see him again.

I hate myself.

I hate myself.

I'm such a dirty bastard.

CHAPTER 1

DOM

"Give me her number." After I've had a moment to calm down, I finally take a seat and decide to work out a plan to see her again. I can't fucking let her go, especially not after the way I treated her.

"It's her husband's number." The tic in my jaw twitches again, and I grind my teeth at his words.

"The fucker's dead, right?" My eyes bore into Johnny's as my words come out with enough bite to let him know I'm still on edge. He starts to answer verbally, but then decides just to nod his head. I keep staring at him, letting him get a good fucking idea of how pissed I am when he refers to that prick as her husband. "So he's not her fucking husband."

"Alright, boss. You got it. I just-" he stops himself and looks at the floor before continuing, "I just have his number. Not hers."

"What's her name?" I'm a fucking fool for not even getting her name.

He shuffles his feet, but keeps his eyes on me. He knows better than to back down, even if I am pissed off. I don't have pussies working for me. I don't fucking like weakness. "I don't know." My rage is getting the best of me. Of course he doesn't fucking know. He probably doesn't even know her dead husband's real name.

"What's his number? Give it to me." Johnny immediately takes out his cell and pushes a few buttons. My phone, still on the sectional, beeps with a text.

It's my doll's dead husband's number. Perfect. I call it right away. Why? I don't fucking know why. I immediately hang the fuck up on the first ring. What the hell is wrong with me? What am I going to say? *Hey, sorry I fucked you like you were some slut. Didn't mean to take advantage.* Fucking hell, I'm losing my touch. "I'm gonna send this over to Tony." Tony will tell me everything he can about this number. From who it belonged to, to what that fucker ate for breakfast the day he died. More importantly, I'll find out who his widow is.

"Johnny, how many of these fucking drops do I have to sit through today?"

"We've got three more lined up, boss," he answers.

"Fan-fucking-tastic." I can't shake my irritation. I need to calm down before shit gets out of hand. I roll my shoulders, throw my scotch back and pour myself another.

"Your ma having dinner tonight?" Johnny asks me like he has no clue. Must be his fucking nerves getting the best of him.

"Relax, I'm just a bit wound up."

"What'd she say to you that's got you on edge?" he asks.

"She didn't say a goddamn thing, Johnny. I'm just curious." He raises a brow in question.

"Her pussy that good?" he asks with a smirk.

"You really wanna push me right now?" That wipes the smile off his face and puts one on mine. I laugh at him and pour him a drink. I walk over to him, a glass in each hand. He takes his drink from my hand and gives a small nod in thanks. "*Salute*," I say, clinking my glass with his

"*Salute*." He takes a small sip and winces as the burn stings his throat. I chuckle and gulp back the rest. I shake out my arms and already feel a bit more relaxed. I throw my feet on the table and get ready to text Tony.

"What's the cheers for, boss?"

I grin and press send on the text. I adjust in my seat and lean my head back on the sleek, black leather sectional. "Just found my new girl."

His brow furrows in confusion and then disbelief, but he's quick to straighten out his face. He takes another sip and walks to the window to look out over the field. It's Sunday, but there's nothing going on today. Team's on break, I take it.

"Been a while for you, hasn't it?"

"Yeah, it's been a bit. I wanna take her on though."

"She into that?" he asks with very real curiosity in his voice.

"Nah, I doubt it; that's not how I like 'em. I enjoy breaking 'em in." I groan and adjust my dick, which is already getting hard again just from thinking about taking a belt to her lush ass. Fuck, I didn't even get a chance to truly enjoy her body. I smirk to myself, thinking of how I'm gonna punish her the second I get her alone for leaving like she did.

Johnny says, "I've been thinking about trying a thing or two, in the bedroom." He looks out the window like he's thinking real fucking hard about it. I snort at him, but before he can respond there's a hard knock at the door. I run a hand down my face and then through my hair. I can't wait to get this shit over with so I can go to Ma's and finally eat something. As Johnny opens the door, my phone goes off on the coffee table. Perfect fucking timing. I don't want to deal with whatever prick owes me money. I lean down to pick it up, and as I do all hell breaks loose. A fucking bullet whizzes by my head, right where I just was.

Johnny's scuffling with the fucker who's screaming for his life at the door. Johnny pushes him down, laying all his weight on top of him, with one hand over his mouth and the other on the silencer attached to the gun. I'm real fucking aware of exactly how the gun is pointed, so I stay out of the line of fire as I jump over the sofa and make my way to the two of them.

Johnny's a pretty big dude. He's all muscle, broad-chested, and this puny fucker doesn't stand a chance. He's putting up one hell of a fight though.

My hand reaches into the waistline of my pants, but my gun isn't there. Fuck! I don't have my gun. I always fucking have my gun, but I belatedly remember removing it so I wouldn't scare off my doll earlier. I look over to the door and it's on the other side of the room. The worst fucking place possible. I keep low to the ground with my eyes on Johnny and this dumb shit. You gonna take a shot at me, you better fucking make sure it takes me out. Johnny carries reverse. I know right where his piece is. I come up from behind him and let him know it's me.

"Grabbing your piece, Johnny." In one swift move I've got his gun pointed at this fucker's head. He looks up with his eyes wide and finally stills, ending the struggle. "Keep your hand on his mouth and grab the gun."

The guy's eyes dart from me to Johnny. I can tell he's figuring out that he's going to die right about now. He loosens his grip on the gun and starts shaking his head and screaming something through Johnny's hand. It's not "help," like I expected it to be. Even if he could scream out for help, no one's coming for him. I've had this suite for years. This wouldn't be the first time some chump thought he'd just kill me instead of paying his debt.

His muffled voice utters a sound that gets my attention. "Johnny, let the fucker talk."

Johnny looks up at me with sweat covering his brow from the struggle. His face is red, and he's still breathing like he's run a mile. I jerk my head to the table by the door and say, "Get mine; I wanna switch."

Johnny rises slowly, grabbing the bastard's gun and walks to the door calmly, straightening out his jacket and tucking his shirt back in. I track him in my peripheral vision, but my focus is on this skinny fuck looking straight into the barrel of the gun I've got pointed right between his eyes.

"Last words?" I ask, closer to pulling the trigger more than I really should. I shouldn't kill him here. Not with Johnny's gun. This fucker brought one with a silencer though. So it's his funeral. And I'll have to fix the flooring. But I bought extra wood the last time I remodeled for this very fucking reason.

"De Luca sent me." He spits the words out with terrified eyes. I smirk at him. Yeah, that's what I thought he said. I don't want to kill him with this gun anyway. So he can talk a bit more. Maybe I'll learn something new.

"Oh yeah? Why's that?" I ask him, switching guns with Johnny and motioning for him to give me this fucker's gun. How damn sweet is that? He comes to kill me; I unload his gun in his head. Seems fair enough to me. The only thing that's unfair is that I'll have to rip out some of the hardwood flooring and replace it.

The scrawny prick is crying his eyes out. The smell of urine hits me, and I look back at him with disgust. Did De

Luca really think he'd get rid of me with this little piece of shit? I squat down to see him better and to put the gun closer to his head. I take a good look at his face and then settle for just reaching into his pants for his wallet. I toss it at Johnny without taking my eyes off this chump. This punk is young and scared for his life, but I don't underestimate anyone. Not now, not ever. You never know when someone might surprise you. And I don't fucking like surprises.

Not like that nice piece of ass today. *She* was a welcome surprise. My dick starts getting all fucking excited thinking about being in that hot pussy again. Fuck. Now is not the time to let my mind go there. Although it does make me wanna end this shit sooner, rather than later.

"De Luca's pissed about the territory, he wants all yous dead."

"All *yous*?" I echo, and arch an eyebrow.

"You need to learn to speak properly, Mr...?" I ask him, but not really. I know Johnny's gonna answer, and he does.

"Marco, Marco Bryant. Twenty-three, and an organ donor." Johnny's confident voice rings out from behind me and ends with a snort. Yeah, these organs are getting donated. I see him pocketing Marco's wallet as I nod my head. *Bryant.* Just like I thought, he's not full blood. No way De Luca gives a fuck about him.

"So, Marco. You need to get your shit together. You think De Luca was really giving you a chance?" Marco starts trembling beneath me, and widens his eyes. He doesn't know how to answer. Fuck, I wanna roll my eyes at this prick. But I don't take chances.

"Don't answer; I don't really give a fuck." I push the barrel of the gun between his eyes and ask, "You got anything else for me?"

"I'll give you everything!" His eyes are darting between me and Johnny, and his face is sweating like he's stranded in a desert in July. Or like he's about to lose his life. I can practically hear his heart pounding in his chest.

"Everything?" I ask with a smirk. He's got nothing that I want. I've got more money than I know what to do with. Unless he's got that chick's number, there's nothing I want from him.

"I've got a house on the southside and forty grand that's-" I pull the trigger before he can finish. I miss the bang of the bullet, but it's better this way. Nice and quiet. I get up quick so I don't get any blood on my suit.

"Grab the list and see if he was one of the drop-offs. If not, this is gonna be one long fucking day." I head over to the bar and finally get my gun positioned right where I like it. That's better.

"Got it, boss. Yeah, he's one of 'em." My chest rumbles with a laugh. "Wonder if he has a history of making bets and he got that forty grand by winning?" Johnny laughs as he picks Marco's head up and starts wrapping it with plastic wrap. Really distorts the fucker's head, but it works well for keeping all the blood from getting everywhere.

"Drop him off at the vet before Ma's." Everyone in my family *knows* someone. My vet was a wonderful addition to my contacts. If you can cremate a hundred and fifty pound dog, you can cremate a hundred and fifty pound corpse.

"You really wanna push it? You know your Ma hates it when you're late." Johnny talks while he wipes up the blood. I flip the scrawny bastard over and pull him by his feet away from the mess.

I don't answer Johnny. I'm always fucking late. She'd be surprised if I showed up on time. I stare at the rag in Johnny's hand that's soaking up the blood. Damn, it's a lot of blood. Never gets old. I stand up from the dead bastard and head back to the bar for a drink. Our glasses are somewhere else, but there's plenty of new ones to fill. And plenty of liquor to fill them with.

This is why I'm the bookie in the family. I didn't really want to be a part of this shit. But with a name like Valetti, this shit tracks you down. "Yours is up here when you're ready, Johnny." As soon as I set my glass down, there's a knock at the door. Fucking perfect.

I walk over to Johnny and pick up Marco's legs while he gets his upper body. This fucker looks small, but his dead, limp body is fucking heavy. We'll dump him in the corner for now. I take a look at Johnny and straighten his jacket.

"You look good, just wipe your face," I tell him and return

to my glass.

"Uh, Dom?" Johnny asks while another knock echoes through the suite.

"What?" I tilt my chin to the door. After that shit, I'm not opening it. I smirk at the thought.

Johnny motions to his hips while looking at mine. I take a glance down. "Fuck!" Motherfucker; fucking Marco ruined my Brioni suit. It cost more than that dumb fuck had in the bank. I look over to his carcass slumped in the corner of the room behind the pool table as Johnny opens the door. With one hand positioned firmly on the butt of my gun, and the other on my drink, I'm listening but I keep my eyes on the dead body in the room.

I'm vaguely aware of the transaction as the pit in my stomach sinks and blood rushes in my ears as their voices turn to white noise. I fucking hate that I was born a Valetti. But it's sure as shit better than being born Marco.

CHAPTER 2

BECCA

The car door shuts as Sarah gets out of the car. It closes lightly. I'm surprised the fucking light isn't flashing to tell me it's not closed all the way. Too gentle. Sarah is too gentle, too nice. We spent most of the car ride in silence. She kept opening her mouth like she was going to say something, but never did. What is she really going to say?

I swallow the lump in my throat and dig through the console for some tissues. I swear to God if his cum has leaked onto this dress I'm going to be mortified. I don't have a change of clothes, and it's not like I can just hide in the car. It's Jax's first game of the season. He may only be three and never remember this, but I will.

I close my eyes and wipe myself, feeling like a dirty slut. I've only ever been with one man. Rick the prick, as I'd recently started calling him. Until he died, anyway. I shake my head and shove the used tissue into the leftover paper bag from Dunkin' Donuts this morning. I crumple up the bag and toss it onto the passenger's seat. Taking a few deep breaths, I open my door and slide out of my seat. No one knows. I keep repeating that to myself as I turn my head to take a look at the back of my dress. Thank fuck there's no mark. Honestly, they'd probably believe I sneezed and pissed myself a bit over me actually having had sex with... him. Tears well up again, and my throat closes. I don't even know his fucking name.

I start walking along the tree line, looking over at the soccer fields. A loud whistle blows through the air and practically scratches my eardrums like nails on a chalkboard. I wince and rub my temples. Jax is at the very last field. Fuck these heels. I feel like a damn moron walking in heels on grass. I nearly topple over pulling one off, but the second is easier. I shake out my fears and anxiety; no one knows.

My heart clenches in pain once again. I can't say I didn't enjoy it. I can't say I never fantasized about being taken like that. Ruthlessly. Being devoured by a man consumed with lust. My cheeks heat with a violent blush. I need to get my shit together. I can't let these bitches smell any blood in the water.

"You're late, Becca," Cynthia says in a singsong voice, but

there's a ring of disdain on the end. I hope she's fucking burning up in that strawberry tweed Chanel skirt suit. Her blonde hair is in a perfect bun, showing off her too fucking large diamond earrings. She's a picture-perfect housewife. The kind of twig who doesn't even finish all of her salad and knows exactly how everything is *supposed* to be done and doesn't mind chiming in to correct others constantly. Yeah, she's what Rick thought he was getting when he married me. Fuck her.

My eyes drop to her heels. All the moms are wearing heels even though they're digging slightly into the dirt. I don't know how they don't fall down on their asses. I tossed my pumps into my bag, and now I'm walking barefoot. As I come up next to them, their lips turn down in frowns. Zero fucks given.

"I had an errand to run. How are our boys doing?" I give her the same fake smile she's giving me before turning to face the field.

"They *really* need to step up their defense. How is Marshal ever going to score when the defense is this poor?"

They're three years old, for fuck's sake. I don't even try to hide my eye roll, not that she would see anyway since now she's texting away on her phone.

I spot Jax running after a boy who's kicking the ball. I pray to God he doesn't just push the kid over and pick up the ball with his hands. Rick and I decided it would be good to get him into sports early. One sport, one language, one instrument. But for fuck's sake, he's only three. I am glad I got him into sports to work off some of that excess energy, but these people drive me up the damn wall. I didn't come from daddy's money like these other women. I worked hard to get my restaurant up and running. I put everything I had in me into this industry. It took ten years to get to this point, and at thirty-one I'm the proud owner of an award-winning Italian bistro.

Jax kicks the ball, thankfully misses the kid, and runs down the field. "Go Jax!" I can't help screaming excitedly and hopping up and down on the balls of my feet. My voice gets the attention of the other moms. I see them smirk and look at each other from the corner of my eye, but I learned to ignore them early on. Mommy playgroups are cutthroat in this social group. I know they talk shit about me. That they defended Rick cheating on me because I work too much, and didn't make enough one-on-one time for the two of us. But they'd be fucking stupid to say that shit to my face.

The thought of Rick hits me hard. My chest hurts, and my heart twists in agony. He may have been an asshole of a husband who was going to try to get every cent from me that he could in our divorce, and try to take my baby away from me, but he was also the father of my baby boy. I smile weakly watching Jax in his little black and blue striped jersey. Number three, because that was Daddy's number. Tears well up in my eyes, and my throat closes as a bastard lump forms. I shake my head and try to think about happy times.

My eyes pop open wide, and my thighs clench. Thoughts

of the bookie rutting into me like he fucking owned me make my heart race, and my blood heat. My senses are flooded with the image of his corded muscles pinning me to the wall, the masculine smell in the hot air, and the sounds of him fucking me. I shift my weight and try to cool down, feeling much hotter than I did a moment ago. I'm extremely aware of the fact that I'm no longer wearing any panties. I was in such a fucking rush to get out of there, I left them wherever they fell. My forehead pinches as I try to recollect what happened to them.

A shudder runs through my body as I remember. *He ripped them off of me.* That was the hottest fucking thing I've ever done. But with *him*? With a stranger? A criminal? I don't even fucking know his name. Shame washes over me, and that damn lump in my throat returns. I never lusted after a man before. Never. School and work were all that mattered. I married a nice man when I finally had life all worked out. Had a baby at twenty-seven. I did everything the exact way my parents would have wanted. My blood turns to ice and I look down at my feet, wondering if they'd be ashamed of me now. Now that my marriage failed, and I've fallen to a new level of filth I'd never thought I'd reach.

For fuck's sake, I let him cum in me. I cringe, but my treacherous pussy clenches. I have to repress a moan, remembering how good it felt. My lips purse as I pull out my phone and text Sarah. She's out getting dinner for Jax and me so I can be here to watch his game.

Plan B ASAP please.

I never thought I'd be texting my PA to pick up the morning-after pill. But hell, in the last few months we've grown close. I imagine we're as close as sisters would be, but I wouldn't know. I'm an only child, and I haven't had any family since my parents passed a few years ago. Just after I found out I was pregnant. Tears well up in my eyes as I remember. I was picking out a cute little mug for my mom to tell her. It was going to have the ultrasound on it. I wipe at my burning eyes and try to return my focus to my little man on the field, but all I can see in my head is a picture of that damn mug. *Grandmom in April.* She would've been so happy. I told everyone we were trying. The moment we got married, I wanted to be pregnant. In hindsight, I shouldn't have done that. 'Cause then everyone asks you constantly, "Are you pregnant yet?" It took a little longer than I'd hoped, but stress will do that to you. And when you work the hours I used to work, well, it's fucking stressful. That's why I got Sarah. That's why I cut back and hired more help. It was the best thing for me, and then for my little man, too.

It was supposed to be the best thing for my marriage. But I don't think anything would've helped us survive. Once a cheater, always a cheater. I'm too fucking forgiving. I never should've believed him. Never should've married that sweet-talking liar. But I wanted a baby. I wanted the whole package, the perfect life.

I didn't want a cheating ass husband who blew his business in a shit deal, wanted control of my business, and then gambled away nearly everything I had. Thank fuck I grabbed a hold of my self-respect and started putting my foot down. It was even better when I started feeling he was messing around on me that I confronted it head on. There are givers and takers in this world. I'm a giver, always have been. I know the givers have to set the limits, because the takers have none. Unfortunately, I've learned from experience. From my shit husband. I loosen my clenched fists as the reality of his death hits me again.

I feel like such a bitch for being angry at him. He's dead. He put me through hell and back, but he's not here for me to be mad at anymore. I'm so confused by my emotions. Six months ago, he let his business be torn to shreds and sold off, then he blew that money on a shit deal. Two months ago, I caught him in bed with another woman. Literally. She had her legs wrapped around his hips and her heels digging into his ass as he was fucking her. On our bed. Since then he'd been trying to get every penny of mine and hired the best lawyers he could to try to get full custody, with my fucking money. But a week ago he dropped dead of a heart attack, out of nowhere. Left me with a shit ton of debt, and a giant mess to clean up. I feel like a bitch for hating him in the end, for being relieved this divorce and custody battle are no longer an issue, but most of all I hate myself for not being more upset with him dying. I literally wished he would die. I was hoping that fucker would drop dead. And then he did. How fucking horrible am I that I'm not more upset? That I don't have more regrets?

Some days I absolutely despise myself.

And then I miss him. I see something, like a commercial for a restaurant we used to go to, and it hits me hard. The tears come on before I can hold them back, and I miss the old Rick. And then I hate myself for missing him. Maybe I've just turned into a hateful person.

Everything in the last year has gone to shit, but not Jax; he's perfect. I keep going just for him. He's my everything. As I watch him stumble on the grass and fall, I swear I see a movement to my left. A dark figure behind the trees. A cold shiver runs through my body as I jolt and stare into the trees. But I don't see anything. My body tingles with anxiety as my heart tries to beat its way out of my chest. I swallow thickly and turn back to the field.

There's no one there. I close my eyes and open them when I hear the women to my right clapping and cheering. One of the boys somehow managed to actually score a goal. I clap and yell and smile at my son, who's furiously waving at me. But somewhere deep inside me, fear settles.

I'm certain I saw something. Or someone.

I force another wide smile for my son and keep my feet planted where they are, but I can't wait to get out of here. I need to shake this feeling.

CHAPTER 3

DOM

"You're late, Dom!" My mom's high-pitched voice hits me with a touch of humor as she flicks a kitchen hand towel at me. "You're lucky I'm running behind." Ma's always running behind. Maybe it's in our genes. The kitchen smells like her signature Sunday dinner dish of sauce and meatballs.

"Sorry, Ma," I say and give her a kiss on the cheek as I pull the flowers in my hand around to the front. "Got you a gift though."

She pats my cheek with her hand and smiles as she says, "Aw, you spoil me!"

"Dante! Why do you never get me any flowers! You should take notes from your son!" she screams past me to the dining hall, and I all-out grin. I love it when she does this shit. Calling my dad out in front of everyone. I chuckle as I walk to the dining room and see the family gathered around the table.

My dad made sure to build this house with a large enough dining hall for everyone. There's at least twenty people in here. And it feels comfortable, it feels like home. I may not like everything about being a Valetti, but I fucking love Sunday night dinner.

"Pops," I greet as I slap my hand on father's shoulder, "looking good tonight." Pops is getting old, but he still looks good. He's got dark eyes, with dark hair that's grey at the temples. I have his high cheekbones and sharp jawline. He looks exactly like a mafia boss. And that's good, 'cause that's exactly who he is. I take a seat on his right, across from my brother.

"What up, Dom?" Vince is two years younger, making him twenty-seven. My chest pains realizing the dead fuck in my office was four years younger than my brother. Marco whatever-the-fuck his last name was. My jaw clenches tight, knowing I gotta tell them what happened. Not here though, not at dinner. Ma doesn't approve of that shit.

"What the hell did I do to you?" Vince looks back at me like I slapped him.

I shake my head and reply, "Not you. I got to talk to you guys later." The room goes quiet as I reach for some butter for the roll that's on my plate. I don't wait till dinner's served. Never have. Everyone else waits, but Ma doesn't mind if I get started without her. I don't know why Ma bothers with the rolls though. I'm the only one who eats them. Everyone else always waits for the garlic bread.

"What's going on, Dom, everything alright?" Jack asks. Jack is like a second father to me. He's just under my father in the business, or family, whatever you want to call it.

"Not at the table." My mom bends down with a hot bowl of meatballs, and places it in the center of the table.

I throw her an asymmetric grin as I say, "Aw, Ma, you know I wouldn't." I take a bite of my roll and lean back in my chair, trying to lighten the mood for my mother. "I love the smell of your sauce, Ma."

She smiles at me and seems to forget the cloud of tension still lingering in the room.

Jack is sitting with his wife next to my brother, but his eyes are on my father. The two have their eyes locked on one another like they're having a silent conversation. I try to stay out of family business. Pops told me I'd take the lead one day, but I passed it on to Vince. He's got the brains and the stomach to handle this shit. I'm more of a numbers guy. I help out with the books, but I like my side business I have going on. It's fun. ...well, most of the time.

Jack's wife, Jessica, gives me a tight smile from across the table. She's new. Jack divorced his wife, and then she disappeared. He wasn't right for a while. We all knew what happened. She got pissed one day, and he didn't keep his dick in his pants like he fucking should have. And she went blabbing about the wrong shit to the wrong people. The thought makes me want to put my roll down, but I don't. After all these years, I've toughened up some. Jessica's only been a part of the life for a little under a year. The women stay out of the business at all times. That's our rule. It prevents the shit that happened with Jack's ex from going down. Yet another reason Jack blames himself. She should've known, though. What did she really think was going to happen?

Sitting around the table are more people in the family. Tommy and Anthony are good friends of mine, but they're also my cousins. They're a year older and a year younger than me, respectively. Although they're brothers, they look nothing alike. Tommy's a wall of muscle. His fucking muscles have muscles. I'd be shocked if he didn't take steroids. I hope he doesn't, 'cause that shit will shrink up your dick. He's a fucking hothead like my Uncle Enzo, so it's hard to say if it's from 'roids or just genetic. The younger one, Anthony, looks scrawny next to his brother, but he's lean and works out to keep himself in shape. His eyes are darker, almost black. Anthony is a sick fuck. Tommy might be the muscle, but when we need to get information from someone, we turn to Anthony. Put him in a room with anyone, I don't care who it is, he'll get what he wants.

Two seats down from them is Uncle Enzo; he owns the bistro and the club. If someone's trying to meet my father, they have to go through my uncle first. He's leaning over telling Jack something I'd wager is a dirty joke, if his tone and hand gestures are anything to go by. A second later, that half of the table is laughing up a storm and my father's yelling out with a grin. There are some others around the table: Paulie, Joe and a few other guys I know. I don't hang out with them really. I do the books like Pop says, and I keep my nose clean.

Pops wasn't fond of me being a bookie at first. He said it's not good to do shit that could bring heat around the family. But when I started making valuable contacts, like my vet friend, he changed his mind. I know he's still proud of me even if I'm not looking to take over his empire. I'm not who he thought I'd be, but I'm still family and still worthy of being part of this particular *family*. Ma takes a seat at the other end and smacks Uncle Enzo over the head. "Hey!" he yells out and rubs the back of his head as everyone gets a good laugh in. Tony's on my right, the nerd of the group and also a lifelong friend. He gets the intel that we need. And that reminds me of my girl. My hands itch wanting to feel her lush ass again, and my dick jumps in my pants. I slip off my jacket and drape it over the back of the chair as Johnny walks in.

He takes a seat next to my sister, Clara. I've been noticing that lately. Not sure I like it. They've been friends for a while, but they seem *different* lately. The only people missing are my cousin Jimmy and his little boy, Gino. Gino's a hoot. His mom's a bitch and is lucky she's alive, to be honest. Not that

I'd ever do anything to the kid's mother, but still, she's lucky.

The bowls are going around the table. I close my eyes and breathe in deep. It smells like home. With the laughter and loud voices of my uncle and father talking over one another, it sounds like home.

And then Ma opens her mouth and ruins it by asking, "Dom, when are you going to bring home a nice girl for dinner?" The room goes silent except for a few chuckles from my uncle and Jack.

"Come on Ma, why don't you pick on Vince for a while?"

"'Cause he's my baby," she says and shoots him a smile and he snorts a laugh in return, but I can tell he's embarrassed, too. Good. If she's gonna go after me, she should be digging at him as well.

"Ma, as soon as I find a keeper I'll bring her home, alright?" As soon as the words come out of my mouth, my beautiful doll pops into mind. She's got something about her I think Ma would like. I think it's her innocent yet confident nature, but I can't tell exactly what it is just yet.

Ma starts to respond with one brow cocked, but I'm saved by little Gino. "Mammie!" The little tyke squeals as he runs in with his little knit hat and thick jacket that billows around him. How can he even move in that thing?

"Gino, bambino!" Ma loves that little man.

I grin at Jimmy and nod my head as he walks around the table to take a seat. He's a tall, good-looking guy, with broad shoulders, and a pretty boy face. "Dom, who am I betting on this week?" I chuckle at him and shake my head.

"You read that book I gave you?" I ask, knowing full well he didn't.

He snorts and looks at me like I'm crazy. "Fuck no."

"Then my guess is that you'll be betting like all the rest of 'em."

The room laughs, and I just sit back in my seat until the meatballs come my way. Ma fries them before she covers them with her sauce. They're so good, but so fucking bad for you.

"C'mon Dom, give me something."

"Don't ever bet against me," I answer as I pile up the meatballs. "There's something for you, Jimmy. You wanna win bets, you stay on my side."

"Dude, just tell me this, New York or Dallas over under forty-five point five?" I shake my head at this fool.

"Giants, over." I lick my lips and slice my meatball as I ask, "How's construction going?"

"It's alright. Same old, same old. Wish I had a fun job, like you." It's important that we have someone in the construction business. Now that we have the vet, it's not quite as important, but it's still good for bookkeeping and all.

"It wasn't fun today." Johnny shakes his head and grabs another piece of garlic bread.

I don't respond; we don't talk about shit at the table. I stare at my food and shovel down another bite. I never wanna get dinner over with, but I've got two conversations that need to happen. One about De Luca, and one about my doll. I'll get De Luca dealt with first. But now is not the time.

"What happened today?" Clara asks, and the room goes silent. She knows better. I stare down at her, but all I see is the back of her head as she looks to Johnny for an answer.

"No game today; they're on break." Johnny answers with a smile and a twinkle in his eye. He's real fucking good at playing it off. Still, she should know not to ask questions. He should know not to bring that shit up. And they should both know not to be eye-fucking each other like that. I look to Pops, who looks exactly how I feel.

"I wanna play game!" Gino shouts from his seat next to Ma. Jimmy pulled a chair up from the corner so he could sit as close to Ma as possible. Just the way both of them like it. The little tyke gets the good mood going and all's well for now, but if some shit is going on between Johnny and Clara, they better square that up fast. I take a peek at my Pops and see he seems to have gotten over it.

But I know he didn't forget.

CHAPTER 4

BECCA

"Four," I hold up my fingers for Jax to see, "little ladybugs sitting on a tree." He giggles and holds up four fingers. I love his toothy grin. We're on his rocket ship bed with his Mickey space-themed bedding, reading a story to settle him down for bed. "Along came a frog, and then there were…" I try to turn the page, but he shuts the book on my fingers.

"Little man-" I stop my scolding as he yawns. He's so tuckered out. He almost fell asleep in the bath, and that never happens. He freaking loves splashing in the tub. Especially if he can soak me. It's his favorite pastime. He yawns again and rubs his eyes with his little fists. A soft smile plays at my lips, and I put the book on the little nightstand next to his bed. His cup of water is there, but I really should take it; I don't want him to have an accident. I lean down and give him a kiss on the forehead. "I love you, baby boy. Have sweet dreams."

"Love you, Mommy." Hearing those words melts my heart, and they get me every time. I rise slowly and walk to the door. I double-check the nightlight before I hit the light switch and close the door. I wait a minute, listening by the door. Some days he's a little deviant and gets up to play, but tonight he's pretty beat. After a few minutes of silence, I walk to my own bedroom.

It fucking sucks being in here. Everything reminds me of Rick. I don't know why I haven't gotten rid of anything. The picture frames on the wall are full of our pictures. A couple are from my pregnancy and Jax's birth. But then there are wedding pictures on the dresser. *His* dresser. I rub the back of my neck and sigh. I should take care of this. I really should. I can't live like this. I fall back against the wall and look around the room. The comforter is a stormy blue; it's what he picked. The rug is the modern shag one he wanted. The furniture was all his. There's hardly anything in here that's *mine*. Everything has him written all over it. At least I picked my own clothes out. Thank God he didn't have a preference for that.

And heels. I refused to budge on that shit. Heels are my one indulgence. I don't care if I spend a little extra on them occasionally.

I turn around and walk out of the bedroom; I'll sleep in the guest room tonight. It seems like every other night this happens. I come to the realization that our bedroom was really his bedroom and instead of dealing with it, I just leave. I cringe as the thought hits me. I'm a stronger woman than that, but I'm so fucking tired. I'm way too tired to deal with this shit. I grin and think about messaging Sarah. That's why I have a PA, to take care of this shit for me. I can't message her this late though. That would make me a shit boss.

I grin as I turn on the light to the guest bedroom. This room is mine. All mine. From the antique furniture and cream paisley bedspread, to the pale aqua paint and plush chenille woven rug, it's all me. I curl my toes in the rug and sigh. I can sleep in here. I should just burn the old bedroom. After I relocate the pictures of Jax... and my heels.

I rub my sore eyes and climb into bed. I need to be up at four to make sure everything's good with the restaurant and that the orders came in. And hopefully Jax will sleep in until seven, fingers crossed for eight, so I can get all the morning shit done before the lunch rush starts. I settle down deep into the covers and rest my eyes. Tomorrow will be a better day. I will make it a better day. I no longer have to deal with any of this shit with Rick. The familiar pain in my chest forms yet again. I'm not sure if it's from Rick dying, or leaving me or cheating on me... or trying to take Jax away from me.

That fucking bastard. I shake my head and push down the emotions. It doesn't matter. None of it matters now. It's all over. Paying his debt was the last thing I had to do.

My teeth grind against one another. It's a good fucking thing they gave me his phone and I had the balls to look at it. What if I'd never seen it? "Fucking Rick," I mutter with every bit of disdain I have left in me and roll over under the sheets.

I pull them up close to my chest and snuggle deep into the pillow top mattress. Happy thoughts. Positive thoughts. *Do good things, think good things, and good things will happen.* I repeat my mantra a few times and then open my eyes. I bite my bottom lip, feeling like a bitter bitch, but really – where the fuck did thinking like that get me?

I throw the covers back and head to the shower. I don't care that it's going to fuck my hair up in the morning by sleeping with it wet. I need a real shower. I need to wash all this shit off of me.

I clear my mind of everything and put a few drops of eucalyptus oil into the back of the shower as the room fills with steam. Deep breaths. Deep breaths. The cream marble tiles on the floor of the stall heat instantly under my feet. I step into the water, letting the warm spray wash away the day. I turn around and soak my hair, breathing in deep. Everything will be alright. Everything happens for a reason.

Just as I start to feel the heavy pull of relaxation, I remember today. I remember *him*.

A soft moan leaves my lips as I think of my dirty criminal. Although I can't, I pretend like I can still smell him on me. I wish I could. The eucalyptus suddenly feels like a bad idea. I try to remember that masculine scent he had, all woodsy and raw. Raw is a good word to describe him. A heat rushes up my chest and into my cheeks as I remember that's how he took me, raw. My fingers brush against my hips, trailing down to my thighs. My lips part as I remember him pushing me against the wall and slamming into me. It was almost surreal. Like a dark fantasy I've dreamed about. I pull my fingers back and open my eyes, realizing where my thoughts have gone. I can't do this shit. It's one thing to fantasize; it's another to indulge. *Indulge?* I shake my head. No, that's not what that was. That was him taking advantage. Even if I enjoyed it. I bite my lip and start washing my body. It's so fucking wrong I enjoyed that. No wonder I'm alone. I start to feel dizzy, and I have to lean against the stall. Fuck. I turn the temperature down and steady myself. I'm just too fucked up for this right now. My emotions are out of control. I don't know what's normal, what's rational, and what is just truly fucked.

Other than me. I was, in fact, truly fucked today. I turn off the water and step out. The bathroom is chillier than I like it to be, but it was a quick shower. I grab a towel and quickly dry off. I need to get to bed. I take out my face moisturizer and the serum for my hair and apply both. As I shut the cabinet, I catch sight of the spot where my birth control should be. I haven't had any for months.

Thank God I took the morning-after pill. And just like that, every bit of desire and heat leaves me. I don't have time for fantasies. I don't have time to indulge in something that would destroy the small piece of me that survived Rick.

I huff and throw on a nightshirt to quickly get into bed. Today was a one-off. Whatever I did today – I shake my head with my eyes closed – it doesn't count. Sarah will never mention it again. I wish she hadn't been there. I wish she hadn't seen me after that. After him. Fuck, the thought of him lights every nerve ending in my core aflame. FUCK!

I bury my head into the pillow and try to forget the shameful desire burning deep down in my core. It only takes the thought of him closing the door on me without a second look to shut down my longing. What a fucking prick. He may be hot and powerful and he may have fucked me like he owns me, but he's still an asshole. All men are fucking assholes.

It's wrong to want a man like him. But I can't lie to myself; I really fucking want him.

CHAPTER 5

DOM

"So tell me what you know about her." I question Tony as soon as I get him alone. De Luca's fucked. He's been fucked. We gotta keep our heads low. Yada yada. Same shit as last week. Motherfucker came for me; I took care of it. Pops is proud, and he's sending a message. Beyond that, I don't want a damn thing to do with this shit.

Back to making bets and hunting down my doll. Just thinking about her owing me makes my dick grow rigid. I shift my weight to cover it up, waiting for Tony to get all the info on the iPad. He takes that thing everywhere. I don't really like the idea, even if it is password protected and encrypted. I told Pops, I told everyone. Apparently this technology is fine, and it doesn't have *everything* on it. Still, I don't like having a device with any information on it pertaining to the business.

I have to admit though, when he hands it over to me and my doll's picture looks back at me, suddenly I don't really give a fuck about the iPad. I read the description and go through the photos.

Rebecca Lynn Harrison. Maiden name: Bartley.

Thirty-one years old. Birthday: January 2nd 1985.

Widow to Richard Francis Harrison.

Married: December 14th 2011.

Died of heart attack at thirty-four years old.

Birthday: May 12th 1982.

Mother to Jax Liam Harrison.

Three years old. Birthday: April 5th 2013.

My jaw tics as I read that part about a son. Kids complicate shit. I can't just keep her to myself whenever I want and expect her to submit without any question.

Owner of Marcello's Italian Bistro.

127 Pattinsons Plaza. Value: Two million.

Owner of two-story family home in Harmony Place.

42 Hills Lane. Value: 600,000.

Recent Legal Action:

Divorce and distribution of assets – dismissed

Questions regarding custody – also dismissed

"What the fuck is this about?" Anger rises in my chest. Is she not a good mother? I won't fuck with someone who doesn't take care of their own. That's not the kind of woman I want.

"Her husband was a piece of shit. I've got his info on there, too." He motions to the iPad, and I suck in a deep breath.

I scroll past a few pictures of my doll in front of her restaurant. *Marcello's Italian Bistro.* I'll have to see about that. I doubt her meatballs are as good as Ma's. I smirk, taking in the façade of the restaurant. I've never been there; never even heard of it. We have our own upscale bistro. But the people who come to us are looking for an experience, not necessarily our food. It's not like Pops isn't known as the head of the mafia. The cops have been on him throughout the years, but they've never been able to get anything to stick. The papers crucify him any time there's bloodshed in the streets. Most of the time it's got nothing to do with us though. Sometimes it's deserved, but it's a rare day the papers get their information right.

So when people come into our bistro, they're hoping to see some shit from the Sopranos or something. The thought makes me chuckle. I stare at the picture of her restaurant. Of Rebecca's restaurant. I like that name. Rebecca. It feels good on my tongue. It looks like a nice place. I bet it's decent inside. But Italian? Real Italian? Nah, I doubt it. I smirk and keep scrolling. I'll have to go in and find out for myself.

I stop on a picture of her holding a little boy in her arms. He must be her son. I look past the kitchen doorway to the den and take a peek at Gino.

"What's Gino now? Is he three?" I ask him as I lean against the granite countertops.

He shrugs as he says, "No clue, Dom."

"Ma!" I yell through the kitchen to the dining room where her and Jessica are having a cup of tea. I know I'm interrupting them, but Ma won't mind.

She walks to the doorway with her hands on her hips and her lips pursed. "Why do you have to yell, Dom? Huh? You can't just walk into the room like a normal person?"

"Sorry Ma, just wanted to know how old Gino is."

"He'll be three in June." She narrows her eyes at me and says, "Why are you asking?"

I shrug as I reply, "No reason." I don't lie to my Ma, not ever. But of course the one time I do, she sees right through me. I guess I don't lie 'cause I'm a shitty liar. Her eyes focus on the iPad in my hands. "Not now, Ma," I warn her. Her lips part and she takes a step back, giving me a look of disappointment.

"I wanna see, Dominic." She puts one hand on her hip, and the other is palm up, extended in front of her. Fuck me.

"Ma. It's just a girl; she doesn't even know me." Well, she kind of knows me, in the biblical sense, but Ma doesn't need to hear that.

"There's a lot of broads out there, Dom," Pops says as he comes up from behind me and takes the iPad out of my hand. He's the only one in here I'd let get away with that shit. He chuckles. "You always go for the challenge, don't you? You can't be happy with a nice single twenty-something. You wanna go for a chick with baggage."

"Dante! A child is not baggage!" Ma looks pissed. I raise my eyebrows and stare past my ma to the dining room. My parents don't fight. Never. Can't tell you one time they ever got into an argument. But Ma sure as shit likes to beat up on Pops. She doesn't let him get away with a damn thing.

"Oh hush, I'm only saying having a kid creates extra work." He hands the iPad back to me and adds, "If he's not looking for anything but a good time, there's no reason to go after a broad who has to worry about a little one." I nod my head, hearing what my pops is saying, but I don't fucking like it.

"What you need to do is knock it off with all the girls and find a good woman to settle down with."

"All the girls?" I scrunch my face up in distaste. "What girls?" It's not like I bounce from girl to girl. I'm not some fucking manwhore. Not that I really see a problem either way. By that I mean I'm not into slut-shaming. You do what you want, how you want. Vince has a fleet of women coming and going. They know what they're signing up for, and I don't give him a hard time over it. I just prefer something different. I like to build some trust. A one-night stand is nothing that can give me the high I need. It's a quick release, and that's just not my thing. I like gaining trust and pushing limits. I enjoy finding out a woman's deepest, darkest fantasies. Hard to make that come true if they don't trust you enough to tell you.

I hear Vince laugh from the den. Great, the whole fucking family is in on it now. He walks into the kitchen, moving to lean against the fridge with a huge fucking grin on his face. I cut him off as his mouth opens. "Shut it." I point my thumb in Ma's direction. "She gets a pass." Then at Pops. "He gets a pass." Then I point at him with my brows raised. "Not you. Fuck off."

"Dom!" Ma scolds me.

"I know, I know." I roll my eyes and pass the iPad back to Tony. "Language." I look at Tony and say, "Email it to me."

Ma looks at me expectantly. "Ma, really." I don't fucking want her involved. This is just pussy. I can't get this broad out of my head. Partly because I want to apologize, but mostly because I want her cunt wrapped around my dick again. And that ass. Just thinking of it makes my dick come to attention. And that's my cue to fucking leave. I did my part; I came to Sunday dinner. I told them about that little shit Marco, and De Luca's bullshit.

I give Ma a hug as she asks, "You're leaving already?" She sounds hurt, and it would make me feel guilty if she didn't say it like that every time.

"Gotta go, Ma; I love you." She gets a kiss on the cheek. Pops gets a quick hug, and the rest get a wave as I walk my ass out the door to my Benz.

Time to go home and really look into this woman. I already know I want her; I've just got to figure out how I'm gonna get her to owe me again. The smirk on my face vanishes as I remember I'm gonna have to address how I behaved the first time. My hands twist the leather steering wheel. I'm not so good with apologies, but I'm sure I'll figure out a way to make it up to her. I groan, thinking up all the ways I'll make it up to my doll.

I can't fucking wait to get inside her tight pussy again. I haven't got anything planned for tomorrow. Well, now I do.

CHAPTER 6

BECCA

I cringe as I take off my heels the second I get inside the house and drop my purse on the front hall table. Fuck, today was a long day. I wince and suck in air through my teeth as my feet finally have some relief. I drop the heels at the front door and start walking to the sofa, but I stop and sigh. Damn it, I can't fucking leave them there. I hate not being organized. I lean down and pick them up so I can put them back in the closet. Back on their spot on the shelf. It'll make me feel better. If I leave one little mess, then it'll just grow. I can't be lazy, it's not like anyone else is going to clean up after me. Besides, it's easier to maintain a tidy home than it is to let it go to shit and then have to clean it all up.

As I slide my Jimmy Choos back on the shelf, I hear the doorbell ring. I look down at my watch with my brow furrowed. It's only five. I have an hour before Jax will be home. I need this time to prep dinner, which today means ordering out, and to go through my emails and payroll. I really do need to hire someone. I pick up my pace to open the door as it rings again. I can't keep up this pace. I can't keep doing *everything* by myself, especially with how shitty I've been feeling. I swing open the door with a sigh and without bothering to look through the peephole.

My lips part, and my heart stills when I see the man on the other side. He fucking haunted my dreams last night in the best possible way. If I wasn't terrified at the moment, my pussy would be clenching in need. He's in dark dress slacks and a crisp, light blue button-down shirt with a dark blue tie. His exposed neck makes me want to lick it and feel the rough stubble on my tongue. As if he knows exactly what I'm thinking he gives me a cocky smirk, which only makes him look even hotter.

I swallow thickly and try to speak. Why is he here? Fuck. Fuck. Fuck. I gave him everything. Maybe he wants more? Maybe Rick's debt isn't completely paid. My eyes widen at the thought. I shouldn't be so turned on by that. I should be scared shitless, and part of me is. But another part of me wants him to fuck me against this wall and have him leave with the warning that he'll be back to collect again tomorrow. I must be fucking sick in the head.

"May I come in, Rebecca?" His smooth baritone voice drips with sex appeal. My core heats instantly. I can't speak, I don't trust my voice, so I just nod and open the door wider. As his tall, broad frame passes me I seem to snap out of my lust-filled haze. What the fuck did I just do? I should've said no!

I start shaking my head as though this isn't real. He turns around in my living room to face me. I paid a designer to make this room look like it belonged on a page of Good Housekeeping. All plush, cream-colored cushions and dark antique finishes. He doesn't belong here. He stands out amongst all the clean white lines. He may be in expensive, custom-tailored clothing, but he doesn't fool me. He's bad. His hair is messy and rugged. His hands are callused and scarred. His smirk is cocky and sexy as fuck. It's like he was placed in this room by accident.

Looking around the room to avoid his piercing gaze, I spot a family picture on the wall and I'm reminded of how tainted it is by my husband – ex-husband – deceased husband. Fuck. Tears well up in my eyes. I can't fucking handle this. I rub my temples. I just want to get whatever this is over with. I shut the door and follow him into the entryway of the living room. I should offer him tea or a drink. My parents raised me right. But fuck that. He's a criminal. I run my hands through my hair as anxiety consumes me.

"Can I help you?" I'm barely able to get the words out.

A deep chuckle rumbles from his chest. He grins, showing off his perfect white teeth. "I think you can, Rebecca." His smile falters a bit before he asks, "Are you going by Bartley now, or Harrison?"

I need to shut this shit down. I don't need someone barging into my life and walking all over me. I'll give him whatever he wants to just get the fuck out. I should've known he'd be back for the interest. For actual money.

A blush travels from my chest to my cheeks. I shouldn't have been so stupid to think that he'd be satisfied humiliating me like he did. My heart clenches. Was it really humiliating? I shake the thought away. I'm sure he intended it to be. Why else would he be here smirking at me like he owns me? Fucking asshole. I clench my fists and push out the words, "How much is it that I owe you?" I have a few grand in the safe in the bedroom. I fucking hope it's enough. I thought all this was behind me. I told Sarah to never speak of it again, and I fucking moved on. It was only awkward for the first few minutes. Thank fuck for Sarah; I need to give her a raise.

He smiles with that boyish charm I'm sure he's used on more than a handful of women and says, "Doll, you don't owe me. *You* never did."

A lump forms in my throat, making it hard to answer, "Why are you here?" I barely breathe the question. The way his eyes narrow and he licks his lips, he's looking at me like I'm his prey. Every bit of fear I had is replaced with pure desire. My core heats, and my shoulders shudder under his lust-filled gaze. "I want you to go." The words come out weak. But I need to say them.

He looks hurt for a split second, and I almost think I imagined it, but I didn't. I saw it. He gives me a tight smile. "I came to," he clears his throat and looks out of the large bay window for a moment. "I just wanted to apologize for the way I treated you." He shoves his hands in his pockets as his forehead pinches, as though he's truly considering something. "I didn't mean-"

"It's fine." My voice hitches on the end. I shake my head, turning my back on him to open the door for him. If he just came to apologize, then he can get the fuck out.

A small gasp escapes me as his hand covers mine and pushes the front door closed with a loud bang. The lock engages with a menacing click. My body jumps from the noise and then from his hard chest pushing against my back. His large frame boxes me in, and my breasts push against the front door. My heart races, and I struggle to breathe as his hot breath tickles my neck. His lips graze my ear as he whispers, "You didn't hear me, doll. I wanna make it up to you."

A wave of heat rips through my body as I close my eyes. The tips of my fingers tingle, and my pussy clenches as his other hand gently grabs my waist and he pulls my ass into his hips. A strangled moan leaves my lips as I feel his hard dick push into my ass. I can feel the wetness between my thighs, preparing me for him. His hand reaches up my blouse and splays across my stomach. "I owe you, doll. Let me make it up to you." His hand gently travels down my side. A shiver runs through my body as he kisses the crook of my neck.

My breath hitches, and the word is on my lips. *Stop.* But I don't say it. I lean my back into his hard, hot body and rock against him. What the fuck is wrong with me? He wraps his hand around my throat. I love the possession. He could break me. He could crush me. He could take me like he did yesterday. And I want it. Fuck, I want it so bad.

This is so wrong. I shouldn't want this. I shouldn't feel like I need him. I shouldn't feel so empty and hollow, needing to be filled. I bite my bottom lip, warring with myself. It was so good. Fuck, it was so fucking good before. I can only imagine how good it would be now.

My head falls back against his chest, and my lips part as a breathy moan fills the hot air. A dark, masculine chuckle leaves his lips and tickles my neck. It sends an urgent need to my throbbing clit. He nips at my earlobe and then pulls it with his teeth.

"You want me, doll?" His question lingers in the hot air. I can't. I can't want this. But I can't say no. I close my eyes and shake my head. Tears leak from the corners of my eyes. I shove my back against his hard chest. He doesn't move. He's too strong.

"Yes you do, I know you do." His voice is hard and

unmoving, like his muscular body caging me in.

I do. I want it so fucking bad. But I push against him again and turn around in his grasp. I yelp as his hand grabs both of my wrists and pins them above my head. His erection digs into my stomach as his hips keep me pinned to the door. He leans into my neck and hisses, "I hate liars."

My eyes close tight, and I struggle to swallow the lump in my throat. I can't explain it. I can't do this, no matter how much my body begs me for it. My lips find his neck, but instead of kissing him, I bite down. HARD. I sink my teeth deep into his flesh to *hurt* him. I don't know why. I don't want to fight him. But a sick part of me does.

"Fuck!" he yells out and pulls his upper body away while his hips stay pinned to mine, and his hand tightens on my wrists. His dick jumps from my attack. My eyes stare at his neck. That's gonna leave a bruise. There's no blood though. Good. I don't want to really hurt him, just...

His hand that isn't holding my wrists touches his neck in disbelief. My breathing comes in sharp pants as his eyes widen. I expect him to hit me. To slap me across the face. My cheek would sting with a violent red mark. I want him to pin me down on the ground, my knees burning as they scrape against the carpet while I struggle beneath him. I want him to rip my pants down and tear my panties off. I want him to fuck me. To punish me and treat me like he owns my body. I scissor my thighs, searching for relief from the heated need of my fantasy.

But I won't admit I want it, because it's wrong.

I swallow thickly as his eyes darken and narrow. They travel along my body with dark desire as he contemplates what to do with me. I'm paralyzed with a deadly mixture of lust and fear. His hand tightens on my wrists while the other wraps around my throat. He squeezes just before the point of too much. It's not a struggle to breathe, but I'm pinned to the door. I'm completely at his mercy. He holds my body still while he leans in. "You wanna fight me, doll?"

I press my lips into a hard line and struggle in his grasp. My body twists and writhes, but it's no use. He huffs a humorless laugh. "All you had to do was tell me," he says and leans in closer and bites down hard on my neck, making me scream out. The painful pinch of his bite intensifies the throbbing need burning in my core. He whispers in my ear, "Say red."

I still with confusion. *Red?*

"Say red, and it all stops. Do you understand?" My eyes widen as I realize what he's saying.

"Yes." The word comes out easy in absolute submission. Hope and lust stir in my blood.

"Say it." His words are hard and short.

"Red." It whips from my mouth.

His hand loosens on my throat and he says, "Good girl, now fight me like you want to." In a flash, he turns my body and pushes me hard against the door. His left hand keeps my wrists pinned while his other rips my pants down my thighs;

the fabric burns across my skin as he forces them down. I think to scream, but I don't.

I don't want to scream. I don't want anyone to know.

His thick fingers tear away the lace scrap covering my pussy, and his fingers dip into my heat as I whimper. "You're such a fucking slut. So wet for me. Wet for a dirty, hard fuck." I hear his zipper, and that's when it hits me. Fuck! He's not going to put on a condom. I start to open my mouth, but I don't. I can't ruin this. I buck my body against his, and his grasp on my wrists slips. I hear him stumble back, and I run for the living room.

My pants fall even farther down my legs and hinder my movements. I trip and scream out, but his corded arms wrap around my body and cushion my blow. He pins me down as I thrash under him. My fingers dig into the carpet. I try to move away, but I can't. I can't get out from under him. I can't turn around.

His blunt fingernails dig into the flesh of my hips, tilting me up. And before I can move, before I can think of a way to fight him, he thrusts himself into me to the hilt.

"Fuck!" he yells out as I moan into the carpet.

I feel the sting of his massive size stretching my walls. I try to get up, but his strong hand splays across my back and pushes me down while his other keeps a firm grip on my hip as he pounds into me. Again and again. My body heats as pleasure grows in my core. He ruts into me like a beast claiming his prey.

"Yes!" I scream into the floor.

He leans down, keeping up his relentless pace. "That's right, doll; you fucking love this. You love me fucking your tight little cunt." His dirty words send me over the edge. My body convulses under him as intense pleasure wracks through my body. My back tries to arch, but he keeps me pinned and pounds into me without mercy. My walls pulse around him, and he pushes deeper into me. I scream into the floor as waves and waves of hot cum fill me. I lie limp on the ground, loving the feeling of being used. Loving how he took everything he wanted from me.

My bliss is shattered as I hear a beep alert that I got a text message. Reality slaps me in the fucking face. I scramble underneath of him to get up. The word is there, ready to pounce, but he lets me up. I kick my pants off and dig in my purse in the front hall for my iPhone.

Running 5 mins late – sorry!

It's a text from Sarah. I check the time. Shit! It's almost six. My hand covers my mouth. Fuck! Fuck! Fuck! I didn't get shit done. I drop the phone and grab my pants, searching frantically for my torn underwear. Holy fuck. Sarah's coming with Jax and his play date. I don't even remember which kid it is that's coming over. Holy hell, I'm a fucking mess.

"Are you okay?" I look up at the sex god standing in the middle of my living room. He just fucked me for a second time, and I don't even know his name. Tears form in my eyes as I shake my head. *Slut.* His word rings in my head as my throat closes, and my chest hollows.

He wraps his arms around me as he says, "It's alright, doll. It's okay."

He doesn't understand. I push away from him. "You need to leave. I'm sorry. I shouldn't-" I can't finish. I don't know what to say to him.

He looks at me like I've slapped him. And I guess I may as well have. But what did he honestly expect? He came here to fuck me, and he did. He won. It's over. I open the front door and stay behind it so no one will see. I lower my gaze to the floor as I say, "I can't."

"What the fuck?" My eyes reach his as he stands in front of me zipping up his pants, and shaking his head. He walks with confidence toward me, and I can tell he's not going to leave.

"My son." It's all I say. It's all I have to say. He stops a foot away from me and looks me up and down. I want to ask him his name. I want to do much more than I can. More than I should. I have to take a deep breath and try to calm myself.

"I'll go, but I want to see you again." *I do, too.* His words shock me. My lips part, and I stand there speechless.

He picks up my phone off the table and says, "I'm putting my number in here. Dom." He looks at me with a smirk. I feel my cheeks heat, and I cringe. That's so fucking embarrassing. I don't even respond.

He puts the phone down, but then laughs and shakes his

head. He picks it back up and smiles broadly at me. "Dirty Dom, since that's the way you like it, doll." He puts the phone back down and then walks to me. His hand cups my face and tilts it so I'm forced to look at him.

He's so relaxed, so at ease. I want to melt into him. I bite my lip to keep myself from caving to him.

He turns his cheek toward me and taps it with his finger.

I look at him like he's fucking crazy. He wants me to kiss his cheek? "You don't have all day, Rebecca; your son will be here soon." My eyes widen. I don't want that. I have to stand on my tiptoes to plant a kiss on his cheek, but I do. I love the feel of his rough stubble under my soft lips.

"Good girl." An asymmetric grin pulls his lips up.

"Becca." I don't know why, but I correct him. No one calls me Rebecca. Only my mother, when she was mad at me. When I disappointed her. I don't want him calling me that. Shit, I'd rather he call me his dirty slut again than Rebecca.

"Becca," he repeats to me. "I like that even better," he mutters under his breath, and then leaves. I watch as he gets into a silver car without looking back at me. I quickly close the door and lean my back against it. My mind replays everything that happened as my fingertips touch my lips.

What the fuck did I just do?

CHAPTER 7

DOM

What the fuck just happened? I went there to smooth shit over and apologize. I start the ignition and run my hand through my hair. I lean back against the seat and take a look back at her house.

A two-story, single family home. Where the fuck is her picket fence?

Her door's closed. She didn't even wait to watch me leave. Probably has to clean up all the evidence that she was with me. For some reason, that really fucking hurts. But then I remember she's got a little boy. And fuck that, I don't want to be here and have to do all that shit. I just wanted to get laid. And I did. I pull out and snort at a few of the houses that actually do have white picket fences.

But why does it feel so... wrong? It was hot as fuck. I've never had a woman who wanted to do that, to fight me like that. I groan, leaning my head back against the seat as I pull up to a red light. That was fucking hot. My fingers graze the skin of my neck. She fucking bit me. My Becca is one kinky bitch.

The cocky grin on my lips slips as I remember how she looked after. Not after I got done fucking her. She was gorgeous when she came on my dick. Her teeth sank into her bottom lip as she tried to fight her need to scream in pleasure. The memory makes me want to fuck her again. Right now. This broad keeps me wanting to go back for more. I shake my head, not quite knowing how I feel about it all.

I feel a little used, to be honest. I fucking enjoyed it, but damn, did she have to kick me out right fucking then? The aftershocks were probably still racing through her body when she shut the damn door.

She should've at least taken me to dinner if she was gonna fuck me like that. I bark a laugh out at my little joke.

Okay, okay. Now I know what I'm working with. If we're gonna keep fucking, I know exactly where I stand with her. I'd be her dirty, little secret. Usually women brag about fucking me. There's no way Becca will.

As I pull up to the house, my phone goes off. I look at the monitor on the dashboard and see it's Vince. I park the car in the driveway, but leave it running.

"Yeah?" I ask him. I don't really feel like fucking around. I want to get inside and look at my schedule. I gotta figure out when I'm hooking up with my doll again.

"We got a problem." I don't like his tone. My blood runs ice cold.

"What is it?" I ask.

"Detective Marshall took Jack in." Hearing that name pisses me off. Jack's ex threatened to go to him. You don't threaten a mobster, even if he's your husband. And you sure as fuck don't use names either. 'Cause that means you've already talked to law enforcement.

"What's he got on him?" I ask.

"Nothing. But we all need to lay low for now."

"Why'd he get picked up?" Marshall is always trying to hunt us down and pin anything he can on us. Every stupid thing used to get us taken in. Now they're careful, since Pops threatened a lawsuit and the judge in his pocket is on our side.

"Expired license." He's gotta be shitting me.

"Are you fucking serious?" I practically yell.

"Yeah, just lay low, Dom," he answers with a pissed off tone. Jack should fucking know better.

"Not a problem." My hands twist the steering wheel. I always lay low. I'm not out there like the rest of them.

"Yeah, it is a problem." My brow furrows. The fuck it is? "Don't you remember what happened yesterday?"

I close my eyes and pinch the bridge of my nose. De Luca. Damn is he a pain in my ass. "That hasn't been dealt with yet?" We have to be careful about how we talk. No names, nothing that could be used as evidence. Just in case.

"Not yet. We have some issues standing in the way, and now this." My fist slams on the wheel. It's not hard to whack a guy. Really, it's not. And the quicker, the better. Which is why it was supposed to happen last night.

"Why didn't the call happen last night?" It's hard to keep the anger out of my voice. Usually I stay calm and indifferent on the outside. That's how I am. That's how I like it to be. Other than with this broad. She's gotten under my skin.

"We got tied up." What the fuck could be more important than taking care of someone who's trying to *take care* of us? I wanna ask him, but my temper is starting to get the best of me. I can't let that get out of hand. I can't slip up on a phone call.

"What do you need me to do, Vince?" I fucking hate this. I hate knowing someone is out there gunning for us, and we're just sitting ducks. My mind flashes with an image of Becca, her lying on the ground, blood pooling around her pale, lifeless body. Even worse, her son. Fuck that. That can't happen. I won't let that happen.

No. No, they didn't see her. Right? There was plenty of time that passed between when she left and that young prick coming into my office. But who the fuck knows how long they were waiting out there?

Johnny looked at the footage, had to cross every "T" and dot every "I." He said there wasn't anyone with Marco. His car was left in the lot. Johnny dumped it, of course. But still, an uneasiness creeps up on me.

My body stills and freezes. I'm not risking it. I put the car in reverse. "I gotta go, Vince."

"Just hang tight and lay low."

"Got it." I hit end and immediately dial Johnny.

"Yo, boss," he answers casually. Too fucking casual for my liking.

"Did you watch my girl leave when you saw the footage?" I feel fucking stupid for not doing it myself. I grit my teeth as I come up to a red light and resist the urge to gun it. *Stay low.* Besides, I just left her. She's fine.

Fuck! What if they had a tail on me? I haven't been paying attention since this fucker is supposed to be dead. He was supposed to be taken care of. Fucking Jack! My fist slams against the wheel as I stare at the longest fucking red light I've ever sat at.

"Nah, boss. I di-"

I cut him off and say sharply, "Do it. Make sure no one followed her. Do it now, and get back to me when you're done. I'm heading to her house now." It's gonna take another forty minutes to get back to her place. At least it gets dark pretty early in the fall. I'll just scout it out, make sure she's good until Johnny gets back to me.

There's a short hesitation and I know he's confused and

wants to ask what's going on, but he knows better than to ask. And realistically, I have no clue what's going on between us. But if they are hoping to get to us, those spineless rats will use any means necessary. Including our women. It wouldn't be the first time a competitor targeted us that way. But I'm sure as fuck not going to let it happen to her.

I pull up a few houses away, park and turn off my lights. I'm glad she lives in a nice neighborhood; my car doesn't really stand out much here. There's a car parked along the curb of her house, but I know she was expecting someone, so I don't freak out. I stay calm. She'll be fine. I'm just gonna make sure she's alright. That's all. I put my hand on the butt of my gun, just to make sure it's where I like it, and get out with my phone in my hand. I flick it to vibrate and I shut the door quietly. Right before I pocket my phone, it goes off.

"Yeah?" I ask Johnny.

"She's good. There's nothing on there." His answer is quick and to the point. I like it.

"Thanks." I end the call and debate just getting back in my car and leaving. But I drove all the way back out here. I check the time on the phone. It's nearly eight. I'll go check to make sure she's alright.

I chuckle deep and low. That's a fucking lie. I wanna see what my doll is up to.

CHAPTER 8

BECCA

I wish this bitch would just leave already. She doesn't even want to be here. She's digging for information. I can practically feel her claws. Her eyes keep looking all over the room, as if searching for some evidence of *anything* to bring back to her bitchy cabal.

Her daughter, Ava, is freaking adorable, but she's not the least bit interested in playing with Jax. Not that it really matters when they're three. But seriously, just fucking go home already. I watched Ava for an hour, fed them dinner – pizza since I didn't have time for anything else – and Cindy was just supposed to pick her up. Just scoop up your tyke and go.

I've had some really fucked up long days today and yesterday. I need to crash. Or go to a freaking mental institution. I'm not sure which.

Cindy's hand reaches out and touches my arm, bringing my focus back to her. It's fucking cold. I should start referring to her as the ice bitch.

She looks at me with a tilted head and a sad frown, feigning actual sympathy. I should hate this woman. She was friends with the woman I caught Rick with. She knew! But then again, they all knew. Everyone but me. "How are you *really*, Becca?" she finally asks.

How am I? I'm fucked. That's what I am. I'm seriously fucked in the head. I hate Rick, yet I miss him. More than that, I feel guilty about my dead husband. Ex-husband. I don't even know how to refer to him. I'm drowning in work. And I'm fucking a criminal who knows where I live. I'm not fucking okay. Nothing feels okay. My perfect world has been torn apart, flipped around and is practically unrecognizable.

But I'm not going to tell this bitch that. I don't even tell Sarah that. I mean, she knows. She figures shit out on her own. Like when she dropped the kids off. She knew something happened. I could see it on her face that she wanted to ask questions, but she didn't. I bet one of these days she's just going to drive me to a fucking shrink. The thought isn't as funny as I wish it would be. Rick wanted to take me to a shrink. He said I was unstable, and therefore should not have custody of Jax. Fuck, am I unstable? No. I close my eyes and turn my head away. I'm handling all this shit as best as anyone possibly could. I'm doing my best. I really am. My hands cover my face. I have no idea if it's good enough though.

Cindy's hand squeezes my thigh. "You can tell me; I'm here for you."

I give her a tight smile. "It's really hard working through the grief and anger. But I know everything will be fine with some time." I pat her knee and say, "Grief is a journey; I'm just moving through it." It's the truth. Well, a partial truth. The slimmest fraction of the truth. But the truth nonetheless. I'm not going to open my heart for this woman. I'm not going to do it for anyone. Not anymore. Just as the bitter thought creeps up on me, Jax squeals and Ava starts crying.

"Jax!" He's got her baby's blanket in his hands. I shake my head at him and say, "Sweetheart, give that back to Ava, please." Calm tones, display behavior you want to be reciprocated. I nod my head and smile. Positive reinforcement. I think about all the books I read when I was pregnant, and it all fucking goes out the window as Jax grins at me and takes off.

Little shit. I smile, chasing him down the hall and scoop his butt up. He lets out the sweetest laugh; it's the best sound in the world. I carry him back into the playroom, lifting his shirt and blowing raspberries on his stomach. I set him down and easily take the blanket away from him. Ava and Cindy are watching us. Poor little Ava has tears in her eyes still.

"Jax, say you're sorry to Ava." I grab his hand to keep him from running. I say a silent prayer that he just says sorry. I don't want to fight him. I don't want to have to sit him on the naughty step and go through all that bullshit.

"Sowry!" Cindy's got her hands on her hips, and her lips are pursed. What the hell? Does she want me to crucify him?

"Sweetheart," I say and hand him the blanket. "Help Ava tuck in baby..." Shit, I forget what she was calling the doll. "What's her name, sweetie?"

"Missy Jane," she pouts, but she's not sad anymore, now it's just for attention.

I smile at her and walk them over to *Missy Jane.* "Let's put Missy Jane to bed." I hand Ava the blanket and she tucks one end under the doll while Jax puts his finger over his lips and shushes. "Good job, you two! You make such a good team."

It feels like a workout, but at least they aren't screaming at each other and pulling each other's hair. Next year, maybe. I've heard of the terrible twos, and the fucking fours. Not looking forward to that one. I put a hand on Jax's back to keep him there.

"Time to say bye to Ava." I smile at the two of them and then Cindy, who's texting on her phone.

I can't help but wonder what she would think if I told her about *him.* About Dirty Dom. I don't know what he wants from me, but my heart clenches at how I kicked him out. I think he came to use me, but ended up being used instead.

My smile broadens, not that Cindy would notice since she's still furiously texting.

I wonder what she'd think about him, and then I realize I really don't give a shit.

CHAPTER 9

DOM

Looks like I got here just in time. Play date's leaving. That sounds fucking awful. At least the parents aren't outnumbered. Two women, two kids, it can't be that bad. The little girl shrieks as her mother tries to buckle her in. She's got a voice on her! I wince at the ringing in my ears. I guess it can be that bad.

At least my doll has a boy. Boys have gotta be easier than girls. I scowl watching the car leave. What the fuck am I even thinking about this shit for? I just came to check on my doll and make a few things clear.

She's mine now.

I guess that's only one thing, but still. I need her to agree to that. And then I can play with Becca and see just how rough my doll likes it. I palm my dick, thinking about that ass. Fuck yeah, I'm definitely getting in there tonight. Women don't usually get to me, but this one has. I gotta fuck her out of my system, and she's definitely down to fuck.

I walk up the sidewalk to her house and stand next to a car, pretending to look at my phone. I've never stalked a person before. That's not what I do. I know a guy to call if I need someone found. But I'm feeling a little awkward at the moment. She kicked my ass out a few hours ago; she's probably giving her son a bath, or reading stories, or just fucking watching Rugrats with him. I don't fucking know. I'm not going to knock.

Fuck that.

I grimace, not knowing what to do. I always have a plan of some sort. But I'm flying by the seat of my pants over this broad. When she puts the kid to bed, that's the time to pay her a visit. But I don't know his bedtime. I don't know any of that shit. I run my hand down my face. Am I really going to creep around her house to figure out if she's putting him down for bed? I think about knocking on the door and imagine her standing there with the little guy on her hip. Yeah, I'm gonna fucking peek. I need to take a look and see what's going on in there. I'm not into playing Connect Four with the little guy. Not when all I want is to get some pussy. She's really gotten under my skin. I need to fuck this broad out of my system.

I walk to the backyard. No fence, so that's easy enough. I slink around the corner of the house. I'm probably looking conspicuous as fuck, but I can't fucking help that. I don't think anyone saw me though. It's pretty dark, but I stay in the shadows.

She's got a nice deck. Real fucking nice. A sunken hot tub, although the cover is carpeted in leaves from the oak trees lining her property. They look like they've been there for a year.

There's a giant trampoline in the back that's covered with netting. I huff a laugh.

She seems cautious. Protective. I like that, but she also seems uptight. Except when it comes to fucking.

My chest rumbles with approval, and I have to readjust my hardening dick. I have to admit she brings out a virile side of me. A primitive need I don't think I've ever felt before. I fucking love it. I'm not sure how long it will last, but I'm sure as fuck going to enjoy it while I can.

The stairs to the deck are on either side - not smart. Anyone could sneak onto her deck and get to the glass sliding doors to her kitchen easy. Someone like me. I keep my steps even and stay quiet as I move up the stairs. I take a peek inside. I don't want to startle my doll, I just wanna see if the coast is clear.

Her kitchen is pristine. Other than a pizza box sitting on the blue speckled marble counter, there's nothing out of place. Steel pots hang above a massive island. Her gas stove is large enough to cook for a dozen people, easy. This woman is serious about her cooking. That reminds me about her restaurant. I'll have to head over tomorrow and check it out. I was too busy today at the office. I cringe, remembering how a jerk-off tried to convince me he needed more time. What he needed to do was stop wasting his wife's hard-earned money on gambling. That's what he needed to do. I'm sure he won't be doing that shit anymore. Not after today.

I take a few steps in front of the glass. I can see the living room from the kitchen, and there are stairs on the right that lead downstairs.

I can't hear or see either of them though. I look at the handle to the glass door and wonder if she'd leave it open. She better not. She seems too smart for that. I take a tug and sure enough, it's locked.

Good girl.

I press my ear to the door, but I still can't hear a damn thing.

I almost leave, but then I see her. I stand perfectly still. I can't even fucking breathe.

What the fuck am I doing? It hits me this very second that I'm gonna look like a psychopath if she sees me. I push my grin down, afraid even that will alert her to my presence. She's making me fucking crazy. But I fucking love it. I never have to work this hard for anything.

A broad smile appears on her face as she raises her hand and wags her finger. Her eyebrows raise, and I can clearly understand the mouthed word "bedtime" as she disappears from view.

Fuck yeah it is. Time for me to take her to bed. As soon as she's presumably gone back to her son's room, I sneak back around to the front and wait on the doorstep. I immediately send a text.

I want you right now. – Dom

I know I'm gonna need to wait a minute while she puts her son to bed. I'm not a very patient man though. I lean against the wall of her front porch and frown at the text. I shouldn't have added Dom. She's already got my number programmed in her phone. I should know, since I put it in there. I roll my shoulders and crack my neck before crossing my arms over my broad chest. Any minute now. I look down, waiting for the delivered text to be seen.

What the fuck is wrong with me? She's got me all tied up over her. I shake my head at the thought, feeling like a little bitch. This isn't me. I don't sneak out to women's houses and second-guess my text messages. Fuck no! I send them a text, and they come running to me. What is it about this broad that has me wrapped around her little finger? Just as I push off the wall and consider leaving, my phone beeps.

I shouldn't. I'm sorry.

I stare at the text. That's interesting. She doesn't want her dirty little secret anymore? No, that's not it. She wants me. I fucking know she wants me. Before I can respond though, another text comes through.

I really can't. I'm sorry for earlier.

Sorry for earlier? What the hell does that mean? For kicking my ass out the second she came on my dick? That better be what she meant. I think about how to tell her she's going to be apologizing for that shit on her knees while she chokes on my cock, but she sends another text.

> *We just aren't good for each other.*
> *I know it's just sex to you, but I can't do that.*
> *It's just that I've just lost my husband.*
> *Well... you already know that.*

This broad really doesn't care about excessive text messages. I run my hand down my face. What the hell am I doing?

> *I don't mean that as a bad thing*
> *it's just too soon.*

I finally message her back before she can continue this one-sided conversation.

> *Stop overthinking it. I wanna fuck. Now.*

She responds immediately:

> *I'm sorry, I can't.*

I smirk at the phone. The fuck she can't. She was pretty quiet earlier. We won't wake up her son. I'll just cover her mouth while she cums.

> *Yes, you can.*

I didn't come all this way not to get laid. And I want that ass. I decide to make it easy on her.

> *I'm here. Come let me in.*

I'm not taking no for an answer. She's obviously uptight,

used to being in her own little world. And I'm not the type of guy she usually dates. That's fine. I don't mind. She's not my usual type either. But this is just sex. Hot sex. I palm my erection. I want it. She wants it. She's just got to get out of her own head.

I grin at her as she opens the door. She must've changed after putting her son to bed. She's wearing a robe now. Black cotton. It's simple and ends at her knees. She's clutching it to her chest as she opens the door for me to come in.

"What are you doing here, Dom?" I don't like her tone.

"I told you, I want you."

She bites her lip and closes the door as I stand in her living room. I take a good look at her. Her makeup's been removed, and she looks tired as hell. Still fucking beautiful, even more so. She doesn't wear a lot of makeup, not that I remember, but without it her natural beauty shines through. Her hazel eyes are a little larger, while her lips look rosy and plump from scrubbing her lipstick off. Her cheeks are flushed, although that could be for a different reason.

She swallows and runs her hand through her hair, looking fixedly at the floor. She looks uncertain. She looks like she's coming up with excuses. I'm not gonna let that happen. I'm not done with her. She walked into my office, into my life. I'm not letting her leave so easy. Not when I've only had a small taste of her.

"Don't say anything." My voice interrupts her thoughts, and

her eyes spark with desire as she licks her lips. Her mouth parts, but my doll is obedient. She presses her lips together and nods.

"Good girl." I step closer to her and grab her hip in my right hand, pulling her body to me and wrap my left arm around her back to fist the hair at the nape of her neck. It won't hurt when I tug it. But it'll give me the control I need to make this perfectly clear to her.

"You're mine, doll. When I want you, I'll have you." She knows the word to say to stop this. But she won't. She wants this just as much as I do. The question is, just how fucking dirty does she want it? I smirk at her and pull her hair back so I can kiss her neck. I run my teeth along her neck and up her throat before squeezing her lush ass. Her breasts rise and fall with her shallow breathing.

I loosen my grip and take her lips with mine. Her plump lips are soft, and mold to mine. She parts them easily, and I take a moment to massage my tongue along hers. She moans into my mouth, and that's all I can take. I pull back and smack her ass. "Bedroom."

She leads the way down the hall and up the stairs quietly. Very quietly. I can tell when we get to her son's room because she looks back at me with hard eyes and clenched fists, and walks with slow, deliberate steps. "Relax mama bear, we won't wake him up," I whisper in her ear and give her hips a squeeze. "I'll just have to find something to put into that loud mouth of yours." Her cheeks flush a beautiful red hue, and her pace speeds up at my threat.

That thought turns her on. I smirk at her back as we near the last door on the right. I bite my lip and come up with a plan. Her panties. I'm definitely going to shove her panties in her mouth. That's fucking happening.

Instead of opening the door, she hesitates and looks back down the hall. I give her ass a pat and open the door myself. At first I'm confused. This can't be her room. It's too dark, too masculine. I just can't see my doll in here. But whatever, I guess if there's a bed, it's good enough.

"Strip, now." I don't waste a fucking second, and I start unbuttoning my shirt and ripping off my clothes.

A robe and panties, that's it. Fuck yes. The simple robe drops to the floor and pools around her feet. She looks anxiously at the bed.

"Uh-uh, doll," I admonish her. "Panties, too. Then get up there and get on all fours for your punishment."

Her mouth parts with a gasp, but she's so fucking obedient. Even while she's stunned by my words, her thumbs hook into her panties and drop them to her feet. She steps out and climbs onto the bed. I groan as she lifts her milky white ass into the air. It's firm, but I can tell a hard pounding will get it to jiggle. I stroke my dick, fuck yes. First I've got to spank that ass for her being so rude earlier.

I climb up behind her and push her back down with my hand. She presses her cheek to the bed and looks back at me.

Waiting for her next direction. She's so fucking good. I loved her fight earlier. But her submission is even better. At least right now.

"Are you going to take your punishment like the good girl I know you are?" I'm so fucking condescending with this tone as I gently stroke and then squeeze her ass. She moans a yes into the pillow. She's turned on and primed already. Her pretty pink pussy lips are just barely visible between her thighs. "You wet for me?" I ask as I gently run two fingers along her lips. My eyes nearly roll back in my head. "You're fucking soaking."

I squeeze her ass firmly rather than spank it. Shit. I forgot about the kid. How the fuck am I going to spank her without making any noise? It's not going to happen. Fuck.

"You were a bad girl today. Do you know why?" I bet she gets this wrong. I bet she says she was bad for fighting me. But that wasn't bad at all. I fucking loved every second of that.

"For kicking you out." I'm fucking floored.

"That's right, doll." I run my fingers down her back and leave a trail of feather-light kisses down her spine.

"I'm sorry, Dom. I'm ready for my punishment." Fuck, she's so good. I line up my dick with her hot entrance and slam in, not at all in punishment. Fuck that, this is all reward. I stay deep inside her, buried all the way to the hilt and give her tight pussy a second to adjust to me. Her tight walls wrap around the head of my dick and beg me to fucking pound into her wet cunt as it squeezes me. It takes everything in me to stay still. Her face is hidden in the sheets as she muffles her scream.

"Quiet, doll." I grip her hips with both hands. I wanna be rough. I wanna fuck her raw and hard into the mattress. It won't hurt her knees now like it would have earlier on the carpet. Although maybe my Becca would like to have the reminder of me pounding into her tight little pussy. I wrap her hair around my wrist all the way to the nape and pull her head to the side, my dick still deep inside her cunt. "Don't make a fucking sound while I punish this pussy," I hiss into her ear. She lets out a small whimper and closes her eyes. I grip her hair tighter. "Open your eyes and watch."

There's a dresser to our left with a big fucking mirror attached. She can watch as I destroy her tight little cunt. My other hand targets her throbbing clit. I smack it a few times and watch as she opens her mouth in a silent scream. Her eyes watch me in the mirror. I lean down and whisper in her ear with one more smack against her clit. "Watch me own this pussy."

With that I pull back and slam into her. Her body jolts forward, her heavy breasts swaying with the harsh movement. But I don't stop. I push in harder, making her back arch. Her fingers clutch at the sheets as she closes her eyes and bites down on the mattress. Nope. That's not watching. As if hearing my thought, she quickly opens her eyes and stares, transfixed on the image of us in the mirror.

I dig my fingers into her flesh and rut into her heat. She's drenched in arousal, making the movements fluid and easy. The smacking sounds of me punishing her pussy fill the room and fuel my need. I grunt as I hit the opening to her cervix with each thrust. Her body trembles, and a look of pain crosses her face. I know she's got to be on edge with a mix of pain and pleasure. The intensity heightening her need to cum. It'll make it that much better when she does. She takes it though, she takes every blow like a good girl.

I keep up my steady pace and reach forward to grab her breast. My fingers squeeze and pull her nipple. I slowly twist her hardened peak, feeling her pussy clamp down my dick. Fuck yeah, I know she fucking loves that. She thrashes and fights her need to pull away while also needing to push back for more. I fucking love that this is torturing her. Her eyes never leave the mirror though. I switch hands, still slamming into her welcoming heat, and twist and pull her other nipple. A small squeak escapes her lips, and she bites down on her arm in response. She's trying so hard to listen. To take me fucking her while being quiet and watching. Her pussy tightens as a cold sweat breaks out along my body. I'm going to cum any minute, and so is she.

"You don't cum till I tell you to," I snarl. She whimpers and shakes her head. "Don't you fucking dare." Her body heats and shakes beneath me, needing its release. She struggles to hold on and obey. I make it even harder. I reach around her hips and run my fingers along the side of her clit. I need to get them nice and wet with her juices for what I'm about to do next. She bites her lips, and barely keeps her half-lidded eyes focused on the mirror.

"I can't." Her voice cracks as she moans her words. I feel her tightening around me. She better fucking not. I gather her juices on my fingers and move to her puckered hole.

"Yes, you can. And you will, doll; you won't disappoint me." Her eyes flash from the mirror to mine. "Eyes back on the mirror." Her eyes immediately go back to the mirror. She's so fucking good. I speed up and love how she has to hold in her screams, how her body fights for pleasure, but she's denying it, waiting for me to allow it. I push my finger against her asshole and slam into her cunt. "Cum, Becca. Cum for me." I slam in again and push my finger against her forbidden opening, waiting for her to cum. Waiting for it to relax, so I can slip it in. I slam into her once, twice, three more times and then she does it. Her mouth hangs open in ecstasy as her body shudders and heats with waves of intense pleasure.

My finger slips in, and she goes off like a fucking firecracker. The most delightful noises I've ever heard are ripped from her throat as pleasure rocks through her body. Sweat forms on my brow as I fight the need to cum. But I'm not blowing my load just yet. I twist my finger and fuck her ass as she relaxes around me, aftershocks rocking through her limbs.

I slowly pull out of her, both my finger and my dick. I'm so hard it hurts. I need to cum. Her eyes are closed, and she's slumped on the bed. Her cheeks and chest are flushed. She so relaxed, so beautiful. I smile as I look down on her. That's a good thing, because she's gonna need to be relaxed for me to fit my dick in this tight little hole.

"Eyes on the mirror, doll." I kiss the small of her back and gently press my dick against her tight rosebud. I give her a moment before really pushing into her. She knows what to say if she doesn't want this. Her eyes spring open, and her hands grip the sheets as she realizes what's about to happen. Her entire body tenses. I pet her lower back. "Relax, doll. Push back and relax." She nervously bites her bottom lip and watches with a mix of apprehension and desire flashing in her eyes. More than anything though, excitement is written on her face.

She's so tight. I push the head of my dick a little deeper and try to sink in, but she's so fucking tight. I know I must be the only one to have taken her like this. Pride makes my chest swell, thinking I'll be her first. I'm going to take her just like this. "Your husband never fucked you like this, did he?" I don't need her to answer, but I still want to hear it. I want to hear I'm her first.

Her back arches and twists, and her body pulls away from me.

I hadn't even gotten the head in, but maybe I was rushing it. I pull her hips back, and she resists me slightly. "You're giving me this ass, doll." I pull her hips to mine and watch as she buries her face in the covers. It doesn't seem right. Something's off. I don't like it. Fuck it; I'll have to wait for her ass. That's fine. I got in a finger today, and I know she loved that shit. She just needs to work up to it. My fingers run along her pussy lips before dipping in. "Your greedy cunt wants more, doll?" I fuck my fingers in and out of her swollen, sore pussy, making sure to hit that front wall and stroke her G-spot.

I don't get the reaction I expect. There's no moan, her eyes aren't on the mirror and she pulls away from me. I still, and my chest tightens. Fuck, she's hurt. What the fuck happened?

I gently place my hands on her hips and try to pull her toward me lightly, but she doesn't budge. My heart clenches, and adrenaline pumps through my veins. Anxiety floods my system. She didn't safe word. I know she didn't. I would've heard her. "What's wrong, doll?" I keep my voice calm and even, but inside I'm freaking the fuck out. I don't like to see women cry. And sure as fuck not because of me.

"I hate you." Her breathy words barely register as she lifts her head from the sheets. Her eyes are red-rimmed and glassy from tears. Her chest spasms as she takes in a shuddering breath. She may as well have punched me in the gut. What the fuck happened?

"I hurt you?" I just don't see how. I don't know what I did. "I didn't mean to hurt-"

"Get out!" she screams with tears leaking from the corners of her eyes, and then covers her mouth with her hand. She winces as her son lets out a wail from down the hall.

I don't know what the fuck happened. I open my mouth to protest, but she moves past me to get off the bed and immediately puts on her robe. She leaves the room without taking a look back.

She hates me? Did it really hurt that bad? It couldn't have. I didn't even get the head of my dick in. I slowly climb off the bed as I walk myself through everything that happened. She was loving it.

Your husband never fucked you like this, did he? I close my eyes and let my head fall back. Fuck! I groan out loud and grab my shirt off the floor. Fuck! How could I be so fucking stupid? I lean my forehead against the wall and close my eyes. I'm such a fucking asshole. She's not some bitch, looking for a night of fun and running around on her husband. She's a widow, for fuck's sake.

I bend down to put my underwear on, trying to think of a way out of this shit. I need to backpedal fast. As I reach for my pants, I catch a glimpse of something under the bed. I sink to the floor and cover my face with my hands. There are boxes under the bed with his name on them. I look on the dresser and see pictures of them. A cute fucking family photograph catches my eye.

I feel like such a prick. He just fucking died. I shake my head and scowl. She doesn't need this. She doesn't need some prick bossing her around and using her like I am. I swallow the lump growing in my throat and pull my pants up. I need to get the fuck out of here.

She deserves better than this. Better than me.

I huff a humorless laugh and push my emotions down. She's too good for me anyway. And I have no place in my life for her. I start to open her bedroom door, but I can hear her humming a lullaby to her little boy. My heart clenches, and tears prick at my eyes. I don't fucking cry. She said she hates me. Told me to get the fuck out. That's fine. I can do that for her.

I take a peek down the hall. The door is only cracked. I clench my fists and walk silently past the door and keep going. I don't look back or even wince when the floorboards squeak on the stairs. I don't stop moving until I'm at the front door. I hesitate, but only for enough time to hear her words in my head over again.

She hates me.

I take one last look at the house before opening my car door. Her picture-perfect home that I forced myself into. I climb in my car and leave her behind.

It's only after I'm halfway home that I realize I forgot my tie. At least she'll have a piece of me to hold onto. Sadness overwhelms me.

I'm sure she'll just throw it the fuck out. I would.

CHAPTER 10

BECCA

I wake up to the sound of Jax squealing into the monitor. My hands fly to my eyes to rub the tiredness away. They're so sore. It hasn't been that long since I've cried myself to sleep. Divorce and death will do that to even the strongest women. So I'm not ashamed of that.

But I am filled with shame.

I roll over onto my back and stretch my sore body. My pussy hurts from last night. Evidence of what happened. I let it happen. I wanted it to happen. My throat closes, and my chest feels hollow. I can't cry over this. I don't even want to believe it happened. I wish I could just forget him.

What's even worse though is how sad I was when I heard him leave last night. It fucking hurt listening to him sneaking out and hearing the door close. I held Jax longer than I needed to. Long after he'd fallen asleep in my arms, I just couldn't let him go.

As if on cue, he screams, "Mommy!" and my room fills with the sound of his little voice. The hint of a smile graces my lips, and I climb out of bed. Time to get ready. I way overslept. But it's Tuesday, so at least there's no weekend rush. I can get him ready and off to preschool before heading in to the restaurant. Sarah will pick him up, and I'll make spaghetti. Jax's favorite. I shake my hands of this numbing anxiety racing through my body.

It's over. I ended it. My heart pains as it twists into an unforgiving knot in my chest. It shouldn't hurt this much to do the right thing.

Why does it hurt so much? I'm so tired of being in pain.

I hate the start of the week. There's always so much shit that needs to be done. I need to make sure everything is correct with inventory first. I've got to order everything by two to make sure I'll have it all by lunchtime on Friday. I breathe in deep. I have my checklist on the laptop. I'm supposed to interview managers and another assistant manager today. But 1 don't have the time.

1 know 1 should make the time because it would really lighten my load to have the extra help, but there's just so much to do. And 1 really try so damn hard to be home every day by five, six at the latest, so 1 can be there for Jax. Of course, 1 almost always have to go back to work using my laptop as soon as he's asleep. But as long as I'm there for him when he's done with preschool and at soccer practice, that's what matters.

1 can't miss this time with him. They don't stay kids forever.

1 park my car in my spot. The same spot I've parked in every fucking day for the past four years, and a heavy sigh leaves me. 1 really wish 1 could take a break. 1 wish 1 didn't have to run myself ragged every damn day. 1 could sell out. 1 could take the money and try to invest it so it would last for us. But fucking Rick got us into so much debt digging his way out of financial ruin. And then 1 was saddled with all the lawyer's fees from our divorce. And then of course when he died 1 had to pay his lawyers that tried to take Jax away from me. That bill fucking hurt like hell to pay. 1 take the key from the ignition. 1 can't stop now. Just one day at a time will get me through. And at least 1 still have my little man. I'll be strong for him.

Grabbing my laptop bag and my purse, 1 swing both over my shoulder and get out of the car. 1 click the button for the alarm and turn toward the restaurant.

A scream tears through my throat as a large hand concealed in a black leather glove covers my mouthb and a large body wraps around my frame. No! I scream and flail my arms. No! This can't be happening. For a moment, I think it may be Dom. But this isn't him. I know it's not him. Tears sting my eyes as my throat burns with a shrill scream. I stumble forward as the man pushes his chest into me and crushes his heavy weight against my body, pinning me to the rough brick. My head bashes against it, and it scrapes my cheek.

The stinging cuts hardly register as he twists my arm. The pain shoots up my shoulder. The black sleeve of the man's sweater slips up his arm and reveals a dark, detailed tattoo of a green dragon wrapped around a red shield. Another man comes out in front of me with a rag. I struggle in the man's hold, trying like hell to get away.

But it's no use.

The rag covers my face, and I try not to breathe.

I hold my breath for as long as I can, but I can't keep it up much longer. I inhale the chloroform into my lungs.

The last thing that goes through my mind as the darkness takes over is Dom. I wish he were here to save me.

My head feels so heavy. I'm so groggy. My vision swirls, and my chin touches my chest. I groan and lean my head back. "Agh!" That was a mistake. My temples pulse with pain. I try to move my aching shoulders, and then I remember. I struggle against the abrasive rope digging into my arms, wrists, thighs and ankles.

A scream tears through me. My eyes open wide, but all I see is black. I'm tied down to a chair and blindfolded. My heart races, and my breathing comes up short. No. I shake my head frantically. This can't be happening. "No!"

Smack! A hand lands hard across my face and whips my head to the side. The sound echoes through the room. I cry out in pain. My shoulders burn from the harsh movement. How long have I been here? Jax. Tears stream down my face. I bite my tongue. I don't know if they have him, whoever they are. I don't know if they even know he exists. I keep my mouth shut. Who the fuck took me? What do they want?

Dom. The air stills in my lungs. Did he do this? My body shudders in agony, and my chest aches with betrayal. I shake my head. He wouldn't do this. But how the fuck would I know? I don't know him. I should've never talked to him like that. My shoulders try to turn inward; I try to close myself in, but I can't. I'm stuck like this.

"Is she finally awake?" My head lifts and turns toward a distant voice on my right. I don't recognize the thick Italian accent.

"Yeah, boss." A very deep voice sounds like it's right in front of me, and I instinctively try to get away. My feet scrape against the floor. Bare feet. It's to no avail. Two large, cold hands settle on my shoulders and squeeze. It fucking hurts.

A deep, menacing chuckle is followed by the stench of foul breath and cigarette smoke. "You're not going anywhere... doll." My stomach drops, and my chest hollows. *Dom.*

"That's right. We know all about your boyfriend." The large hands try to pull me forward, which only causes the searing pain to shoot up my shoulders and make me wince.

The other voice that sounded so distant before rings out very clear and very close, "Just answer our questions and we'll let you go." A hand reaches out and cups my face. I flinch from the sudden touch, and I'm rewarded with another hard slap. I scream out again, against my will.

"He's not my boyfriend." I barely get the words out. They have the wrong person. I don't know him. I only know where his office is, and his first name. Shame floods me again. I feel like a fucking whore. A stupid slut about to get murdered because some asshole made me hot and I gave into temptation. This is what happens when you're bad. This is where you end up.

I try to keel over as a solid fist lands hard in my gut. The need to vomit floods my system, and pain radiates from my stomach to my back. Holy fuck that hurt.

"Don't fucking lie to us!" The other man, Distant Man yells at me. Tears fall freely as I gasp for air.

"Be a good doll, we need to know where Dom keeps the files for his daddy."

My head shakes vigorously. "I don't know. I swear I don't

know." My heart hammers in my chest, beating furiously as if trying to escape. I wait in the silence for something, for anything.

A hard punch lands on my jaw. My bones crunch, and I swear something cracks. I sob uncontrollably from the pain.

"You do know. There's no reason to keep it from us. Just be a good doll. We saw you bring him the money. When he took it, where did he put it and where did he write down the drop? Where does he keep that pad?"

A loud ringing noise sounds in my head. White noise. It's so loud it nearly drowns out their words. I don't fucking know. I swear to God I don't know. I think back to what happened. I try to remember. There was no pad. I think he just tossed the money on the table. I don't remember. I open my mouth to plead with them, but it burns with pain. I shake my head and plead with them, "I don't know. Please. Please let me go."

I whimper through the pain and prepare for another blow. And it comes almost immediately, landing hard in my gut again. I try to crumple over from the agonizing pain, but I can't. Blood spills from my mouth as I cough it up.

They're going to kill me. I don't know what to say. I don't know how to save myself.

Tears burn my eyes as my head starts to sway. *Dom. Dom, please save me.*

My head hangs low as my breathing comes in ragged pulls. He's not going to save me. Knights in shining armor don't exist. And even if they did, he wouldn't be one of them.

CHAPTER 11

DOM

I wake up to my fucking phone going off. I feel like hell. I drank a bottle of Jack last night, and I'm really feeling it. But I don't even fucking care. I feel like shit. Maybe if I drink enough I'll convince myself the hangover is why my chest aches and the fucking scowl won't leave my face.

I swallow hard. I don't give a shit about Becca. I just wanted to fuck that sweet ass of hers. I probably only wanted her because she was such a challenge. I shake my head, slowly so I don't make myself any dizzier than I am. That's all it was. She was just a bit harder to get. That's the only reason I wanted her. The only reason she got under my skin.

"This better be good." I answer the phone with a pissed off tone clear in my voice. I don't feel like doing shit today. I half hope that someone comes without their money. No, fuck that. I'll just go to the gym. It's been a while since I've really pushed myself with the punching bags.

"Boss." I jackknife off the bed at Johnny's tone and wait silently. Something's wrong. I don't like how long he pauses. I can hear him taking in a heavy breath.

"Spit it out." I can only imagine it's about Vince. They must've got him on some fucked up charge.

"We gotta message, boss. I don't know how they found her." My heart drops like a fucking anchor. He quickly adds, "I swear there was nothing on the tapes. I don't know how they got her." His voice raises with anxiety.

"Tell me everything, Johnny." I'm calm. Deadly calm. Suddenly, I don't feel a fucking thing from my hangover. All I see is red.

"I got a text with a video. They have your girl, Rebecca."

"Who and where?" That's all that matters. I just need that info, and I'll get her back. She's mine. I don't give a fuck what she said last night in the heat of the moment. I don't give a fuck if she pushes me away again.

She's mine.

De Luca." I hear Johnny swallow, and that pisses me off. I wait for more while I climb out of bed and throw on the first clothes I find. Sweats and a white tee.

I snarl into the phone, "Where!" He better fucking know.

"We're on it now." My hand tightens around the phone, and I have to close my eyes. My shoulders rise and fall with my angered breaths.

"Someone decided to send us a message. To send *me* a message. And they didn't give any instructions? You aren't able to track the message?"

"It-It's just a video." My blood turns to ice. I glossed over it earlier in my haste when he first mentioned it, but a video means there's something to see. Fuck, no. I wait for more. I don't want to ask.

"They roughed her up, Dom." I can't breathe. I swallow down my heart, which feels like it's trying to climb out of my throat.

"She alright, Johnny?"

"She'll be alright. I promise you, Dom. We'll get her back, and she'll be alright." I wanna ask, but I can't. I just need to get to her. I need to see for myself.

"What about her son?" A panic spreads through every inch of me. He's just a child. They better not have touched him.

"Preschool. He's still in class."

"Get him out now. Give him to Ma, and don't let either of them out of your sight. You hear me, Johnny?"

"I got you, boss. I'm on it." Damn right he is. No harm is coming to her son. No one's hurting him. Over my dead body.

"We've got to find Becca now, Johnny. How long ago did

the video come in?"

"Fifteen minutes." He's quick to answer.

"How long does Tony need?" I ask with a calmer voice than I thought I could manage. I shove my shoes on and walk out the door with my keys in my hand. I don't know where to go. I don't know where she is. But I can't fucking sit around just waiting. I need to do something.

I'm the reason she's in this mess.

"Any minute. We'll know any minute now," he answers.

"I'm calling Tony. Call me the second you hear anything."

"I will, boss."

I hang up the phone and quickly dial Tony's number. As I listen to it ring, the full weight of everything crushes my chest.

It's my fault.

I led them to her.

I must have. I couldn't stay away. I ruined her.

My eyes close as the phone goes to voicemail. Because of me, she may be dead right now.

"You sure this is it?" I've got two guns on me in holsters, and another in my lap. I chamber the round and lean forward in my seat, looking at the rundown warehouse. They better fucking be in there. It's been forty minutes. That's too fucking long. I watched that video over and over, looking for any kind of clue. My gut sinks, and my fists clench. My poor Becca. She doesn't deserve this shit. I got her into this mess, and I'm gonna get her out.

"This is it, boss," Johnny answers. Vince leans between the two front seats as the car behind us parks.

"Time to kill some De Luca fuckers."

"Let's go." I'm the first out of the car. If they've got eyes on the parking lot, they're gonna see us coming. There's no way around it. It's a warehouse in the middle of nowhere on a huge concrete pad with a runway for planes. There's no hiding. No getting in or out undetected.

I hear the guys get out and come up behind me as another one of our cars pulls in. I don't wait though. I've waited long enough. All of us will come. The entire family is coming to kill these fuckers. You don't mess with one of us and get away with it. We'll find you. We'll hunt you down, and make you pay.

That's what we do.

Jack is the only one not here. But he'd be here if he could. I know he would.

We form a V, with me leading the way to the large steel double doors. There's a chain and a lock on them. Anthony comes up behind me with the bolt cutters while we all keep our guns raised. The heavy steel chain drops to the ground with a loud clank, and he quickly bends and pulls it away so I can pull the doors apart. They open with a loud groan.

They definitely know we're here.

A cold sweat breaks out across my body. They better not have touched her. That image that flashed through my mind yesterday, of her cold and dead on the ground, flashes into my vision again. I try to blink it away, but it won't disappear. I shake my head and grind my teeth, keeping my gun held high. The huge room is empty, with concrete floors that are rundown, but bare. No place to hide. Which is good and bad. It's two stories with a thin hall lining the upper level. It's made of rickety wire mesh flooring so each inch is visible. Six doors are on each level, with two on each side and the back wall.

She's behind one of them. Twelve doors to look through.

My gun moves to each door, each corner. Empty.

"Start at the left. Bottom floor," I call out with determination and confidence.

"We splittin', Dom?" Pops' voice rings out, but I shake my head. I'm calling the shots. My problem, and my girl. I'm grateful Pops is ready to back me up. I don't know how many of them there are. I want our numbers high.

I lower my gun as I reach the first door. I look back at the crew as I test the handle. Locked. I bet they're all fucking locked. They're steel doors. Not fucking easy to break down, but we got this.

I put my gun up to the keyhole and fire. Once, twice, three times. I give it a hard kick, and it jostles slightly. Another shot, and another kick. Everyone has their guns ready to fire as the doors open. They swing open with a bang, crashing into the walls. Boxes are piled high, nearly to the ceiling in several rows. I take a step in with caution, keeping my gun in front of me as I sweep the room. But a faint muffled sound from a distance makes me stop.

I motion for everyone to be still. I swear I heard something. I swear I did. I almost move forward, but then I hear it again. She's not in this room. I hustle my ass past everyone and move on to the next door. My Becca. I hear the sound clearer as I reach the door in the back left corner.

Locked.

Bang! Bang! Bang! I kick it open with no mercy, making my leg scream in pain. Again I fire, and then so does Johnny. We fire together, kick together. The door swings open, and my heart stops. My Becca is hanging upside down, tied up by her ankles over a sink to the right of the room. Her head has her just barely balanced on the edge of a sink that's overflowing. Her hair is soaked.

They left her to drown. They tied her up, and put her head in a sink and filled it. As I take in the sight of her, she slips and her head falls back into the water. I run to her as her body thrashes, and she tries to swing herself to the edge again. I pull her head out as soon as I get to her. Guns fire around me. I don't even know where mine is. I don't bother looking up. A bullet whizzes by my head as men shoot. My family and others return fire. Footsteps ring out on the steel stairs at the back of the room. More gunshots. But all I can really hear is my doll breathing, gasping for air.

My fighter. My survivor. I rip the soaked blindfold off her eyes and turn off the faucet.

"It's alright. I got you."

"Dom!" she screams out, and sputters up water.

"It's me, doll. I got you." She shudders in my arms as I lift her weight up and try to cradle her body as best I can. My entire body is trembling. Loud, heavy footsteps race toward me. The screaming has stopped. The guns aren't firing anymore.

"They got away, boss!" I barely hear Johnny yell. I don't care.

"Jax?" Becca's head falls back, heavy against my arm. She shaking from the freezing water. Her skin is ice cold and pale. Her teeth chatter, and her eyes refuse to focus on me.

"He's safe, doll. You're both safe. I got you."

At my words, her body goes limp. Her eyes close. Fuck no. I jostle her in my arms, but she's still.

"Help her!" I hold her closer to me and shake her body to try to wake her as I scream. "Somebody help me get her down!"

CHAPTER 12

DOM

"You sure, Dom?" Jack's voice echoes in my head, and I scowl.

I want to smash his fucking teeth in. I get that his woman, his wife, was ready to rat on him. I fucking understand that. But this isn't *his* woman. Becca isn't a rat. I got her into that shit. She's not at fault in any way.

And what he's implying is unforgivable. My voice is low and deadly as I turn to face him and stare straight into his eyes with my hard gaze. I want what I say to be heard and understood. "If anyone touches her, or implies that any harm should come to her or her son, I will slit your fucking throat open."

"Just calm down, Dom." I look at my father like he's the one who said it, because he's keeping me from destroying Jack. My fists are clenched so tight my knuckles are white. How could he fucking imply that we should kill her?

"She's just seen a lot is all." He leans back against the bookshelves in the office, and I turn my head slowly to stare him down. Vince, Pops, Jack and I are in the office. Pops' office. It's a dark room with thick curtains and dark chestnut bookshelves lining the walls. They're filled to the brim. Pops loves to read, but he also likes to hide shit. I know some of the books are for his secrets. I just don't know which books, or which secrets.

Vince paces by the door with his hands in his pockets, head bowed, staring at the antique rug as he walks. He doesn't look up to respond to Jack, "She hasn't even come to. We don't know what she's seen."

"She was conscious when we were shooting. It doesn't matter that we saved her. She could blab. She could sell us out."

My father's hands come down hard on my chest and then move to my shoulders, shoving me into the seat in front of his desk. My breath is caught in my throat, and adrenaline courses through my blood.

"That's enough, Jack!" he yells at Jack, but his eyes are on me. I can feel them boring into me, but I'm not looking back at him. My eyes are shooting daggers at Jack. I fucking told him to shut his mouth. I don't give a shit that he's the underboss. Pops knows it. Jack's days are numbered. I won't allow it. I won't allow anyone to keep breathing if they so much as think of touching my girl.

I shove Pops away and sit back in my seat, crossing my arms. I can't turn my face neutral. I look pissed 'cause I am pissed. But I'll bide my time, I'll wait. But I'm not going to let De Luca live.

"You need to calm down, Dom; just think this through." My father's voice is calm and even. My brow furrows, and I glare at him. He can't be fucking serious. A look of shock crosses his face as he says, "Between you and Jack. Just calm down, think it through."

My tense shoulders relax slightly. I nod my head. He means me fucking up Jack. Thank fuck. I don't know what I would do if he was talking about my doll. I swallow thickly and spear my hands through my hair and then grip it while I lean back in my seat. I stare blankly at the office ceiling.

I just can't get the image of her hanging there out of my head. Her face is bruised. Her eye, her cheek. She obviously hit her head more than a few times trying to balance herself on the edge of that industrial steel sink. But it's more than that. The bruises, the blood, they really fucked her up. All because of me.

She's in my bedroom. My old bedroom at my parents' house. Just a few doors down from Pops' office. She hasn't woken up yet, and that scares the shit out of me. Her skin was ice cold and pale. When the doctor stripped her down I saw the stab wounds on her legs. They didn't show any mercy. Tears prick at my eyes, but I will them down. It's all because of me. 'Cause I couldn't keep my dick in my pants.

Jax is downstairs playing with Gino. I'm glad the two of them hit it off. Jimmy brought some remote-controlled monster trucks over, and the kids are crashing them into each other. He keeps asking for her, looking around all worried. Ma's got it taken care of though. I'm sure as hell not letting him see his mom like that. I don't want to scare him. I have to protect the little guy as best I can. Luckily Paulie's the only one those fuckers managed to hit, and it was only his leg. Doc took care of that with some quick stitches. A few days off and some whiskey will have Paulie good as new.

"What you need to be worrying about is De Luca and his gang." Pops' voice rings out through the office.

They fucking got away. They were waiting, ready to ambush us. But they didn't expect the numbers. They fled like the cowards they are. We got one of theirs. But you can't question a dead body. We know their territory though. We know where they hang out. It's fucking over.

"If I'd been there I would've told you guys to split." Jack decides to chime in again. Silence greets him. He's not the boss. He knows it, and so does Pops. But for some reason, my father lets him get away with that shit. "Someone always needs to be outside."

"If we'd split up, they wouldn't have run. But then we wouldn't have had the numbers." I finally look back at him. "I made that call, and I'm fucking good with it." I sit forward in my seat. "Pops was there," I look at my father, "and if he wasn't good with it, he would've said so." My father nods once in agreement. "If we're going to go in for the kill, it'll be on our terms. We were only there to get Becca. Nothing else."

Pops squeezes my shoulder and walks around to sit at his desk. He sinks into the leather wingback chair and then clasps his hands and rests his elbows on the mahogany desk. His fingers steeple and the tips rest at his lips. "We had to lay low because of you, Jack. We don't now."

I shake my head. "I'm not ready. I'm not going anywhere until I know she's alright."

"Since when do you come on hits, Dom?" It's not a question. Well, that's not quite the question he's asking, anyway. He knows there's no way I'm not going after them. But I never have before. I don't work the streets. I have my own business. I'm only in this family because he runs it. I have my bookie business, and that's good enough for me. I work the *familia*'s books and that keeps me in, but that's it.

"Things change." I can't look him in the eyes.

A knock at the door interrupts us. "Enter," Pops says, pausing a conversation I'm not really sure I want to have.

The doctor walks in and gently shuts the door behind him. He's an older man with short white hair and pale blue eyes surrounded by well-earned wrinkles. His glasses make him look distinguished even if he is wearing faded jeans and a thin V-neck sweater.

This isn't the first time he's been here, and it won't be the last. Nearly a decade ago, his son got into problems with a gang on the west side. He begged my father for help. Pops knows a good man when he sees him. That, and it's nice to have a doctor available for house visits on short notice for cash payments.

"She's stable and from what I can tell, her injuries are purely external."

"Is she going to be alright?"

"She'll be perfectly fine."

"Did they-?" I can't finish the question. I swallow thickly and search his eyes. He knows what I'm asking.

"The rape kit came back negative." I cringe at his answer but nod my head and let out a breath I didn't know I was holding. I'll never forgive myself for what they did to her. But I am relieved to know they didn't abuse her like that. She deserves better. She sure as fuck deserves better than me, but after what happened, I can't let her go just yet. They know where she lives. Where she works. The doctor and Pops have a few words, but I don't listen. I'm just focused on the fact that she's alright.

Right now she's alone though. I don't like that. I want to be there when she wakes up. I stand up, ready to go see her.

"Where are you going?" Jack asks me as I grab the door handle.

Where the fuck does he think I'm going? I stare at him for a minute, just so he can squirm under my gaze. I didn't forget what he said. And he sure as shit better not forget what I told him. After a moment I leave, shutting the door a little harder than I should.

I wish Jack's fucking head was between the door and the frame. I shake off my anger and try to calm myself. If she's awake, she's not gonna like me storming in there with a temper.

I open the door slowly and walk into my childhood bedroom. Not that it looks like one. Statistics books and other textbooks line the back of my desk, lined up in a neat row. Other than the books, the desk is cleared off. Exactly how I like it. The desk is solid maple and stained dark espresso in color. It's modern, and reflects the rest of the furniture in the room. My sheets and comforter are perfectly white, and the walls are a cool grey. The only personality is provided by a simple framed, enlarged photograph on the wall. It's an abstract shot with bursts of colors. I don't know why I like it. But I do. Other than the framed photograph, my room displays order and discipline. It's how I grew up. It's how I stayed out of the mafia.

Lying under the sheets is Becca. The white sheets bring color to her complexion. I'm grateful for it. She's completely still with her arms placed at her sides, and her eyes are closed. Without the color, she would look dead. I pull the desk chair to the side of the bed and sit next to her, taking her hand in mine. She's warm. I watch her chest rise and fall gently. My heart seems to slow to beat in time with hers.

Bruises still cover her face and arms and the rest of her body. Even worse, the rope burns on her wrists may actually scar. On the nightstand next to the bed are ointments and bandages. The doctor applied them before he left, but I'll take care of her from here on out. I'll make sure this doesn't scar her. Not in any way. She inhales a deep breath and winces in pain. I know she's on pain meds, but maybe not enough.

"Becca?" My voice is hopeful, just as I am. I need her to wake up. I need her to tell me everything. And I need to apologize.

Her eyelids slowly open in a daze, either from a concussion or the meds, or maybe just exhaustion. I take her hand to my lips and kiss her knuckles, keeping my eyes on her face. Watching her every movement.

"I'm here, doll. You're alright." Her eyes blink slowly and she turns her head, rubbing her cheek against the pillow. It takes a moment, but her eyes find mine. They seem to widen slightly, but she's still dazed.

"Jax?" She barely breathes his name.

I give her a reassuring smile. "He's downstairs playing. He has no idea." She closes her eyes and lets out a long exhale before slowly opening them again.

"Thank you." Her hand weakly squeezes mine. Her head turns, and she winces in pain again before staring at nothing.

"I'm sorry."

"You have nothing to be sorry for." My throat starts to close, so I grunt a cough and clear my throat. "It's my fault, doll. I'm sorry." I fucking hate that I'm apologizing. Not that I shouldn't be, but that I've hurt her again.

She shakes her head slowly and then takes a deep, shuddering breath. She rubs her eyes and tries to get up, but I gently push her shoulders down.

She looks at me like I punched her. "I need to get Jax."

"He's downstairs." She's fucking crazy to think she's going anywhere.

"I need to take him home." Fuck that. That shit's not happening.

"You'll come home with me tonight." I'm already dreading the drive, but we aren't staying with my parents. I have a house and a room for her and Jax. I'll take care of them.

She pushes me away, but then seems to consider my words. "Are they going to come back?"

"They will never hurt you again. I'm going to find them. I'll take care of this." Tears well in her eyes.

"I can't just stay here." Her voice is pained.

"Don't worry, Becca. I'll take care of everything."

She shakes her head and says, "You don't understand. I have work; Jax has school and soccer. I have a life." She takes in a strangled breath. "I had a life." Her knees pull into her chest, and she rolls over and buries her face in her hands. She sobs, and I don't know what to do. I don't know what to tell her.

She can't just go to work. She wouldn't want to if she got a look at herself anyway. She can't go home. I can't let her out of my sight. I'm not going to give them another chance to hurt her.

"Phone!" She pops up too quickly for me to stop her.

"Doll, lie back down." I try to get her to lie back, but she's on her feet and looking around the room for her clothes. She's holding a sheet draped around her.

"I need my phone and my clothes." What the hell is wrong with her?

"You need to relax and take it easy."

She shakes her head, but at least she stops in her tracks. "I need my phone." She just keeps repeating herself. I finally pick it up off the bedside table and hand it to her.

"Where are my clothes?" she asks with her eyes on her phone.

"Trashed." Her eyes shoot up at me. "I'll get you new ones."

"You don't need to do that. I can get my own." The way she says it makes my chest hurt. "I just need to get back. I have so much I need to catch up on."

As I stare at her like she's crazy, the doctor knocks gently and walks in immediately after. His bushy white eyebrows raise when he sees Becca out of bed.

"Mrs. Harrison?" he asks with skepticism.

She stares at him with wide eyes until her phone beeps in her hands and she starts typing away. There is obviously something very fucked up with her head right now.

"Do you mind if I ask you a few questions? I need to do a small physical as well now that you're awake."

"I'm fine. Really, I'm fine." I quirk a brow at her. Who the fuck says she's fine after going through that shit? And who the fuck is she texting? I stand up and grab her by the waist to pull her back to the bed. She goes rigid in my arms, but she doesn't fight me.

"You need to lie down, doll. You're not fine." I lay her on the bed and she immediately sits up, covering herself with the sheet, phone still in hand.

"Who are you texting?" I finally ask, and she looks back at me with defiance.

"Sarah. I needed to make sure everything is running smoothly. And it's not!"

"Mrs. Harrison-"

"Stop calling her that!"

"Stop calling me that!" We snap at the doctor in unison. Well at least we're on the same page about something.

"Rebecca, then?"

"Becca." I correct him before she opens her mouth.

"Ah. Becca, may I take your vitals and ask you a few questions?"

She keeps her lips pressed together and nods slightly. Why is she acting like this? She just got abducted and beaten, almost murdered. Is she hiding something? She's got to be holding something back. She lays the phone on the bed and I immediately snatch it. A click of the home button takes me to her security code screen. I start to ask her, but then I remember her son's birthday from the info Tony gave me. The day after my mother's birthday. I click 0405 on the screen, and it opens. Her eyes widen, and her jaw juts out.

"Don't text her back yet. I'll figure out why." She starts breathing heavy. "I'll come up with a lie."

I read through the few dozen texts from "Sarah PA." Holy shit. Who the fuck has this many questions in only a few hours? The last one is, "where are you?!?" And Becca's already responded to all of the other requests.

"You're not going to tell her anything." I put the phone in the pocket of my sweats and cross my arms. "You're going to lie there and get your physical and then rest so you can get better."

"I'm fine." Doctor Koleman's busy reading her pulse and ignoring us.

"You aren't fine." I don't want to recount everything that happened today, but how the fuck could she think she's fine?

The doctor takes the stethoscope from around his neck and instructs her to sit and breathe. At least she's listening, even if she's ignoring me.

"Becca, how are you feeling?" he finally asks, taking a seat in the chair I left by the bed.

"Don't say fine." I cut her off with a hard glare as she opens her mouth.

"I feel sore, especially my ribcage." She speaks calmly, but the doctor cuts her off.

"Two of your ribs are fractured. You'll have to rest up to help them mend." She stares at the doctor with a look of confusion before shaking her head.

"No, I'm fine." Her voice is small and laced with disbelief.

His brow furrows. "I'm certain they're fractured. You're on pain medicine at the moment, codeine. It's going to take at least six weeks to heal properly. You don't have to rest in bed all day, that's fine. But you do need to take it easy and make sure to do some deep breathing every two hours to prevent any further damage to your lungs."

She breathes in deep, as if testing his words. Her eyes fall to the floor.

The doctor continues, "Other than the fractures to your ribs, you have some serious abrasions on your ankles. I've left ointments here. You're going to want to keep them covered when you shower, but gently wash them after and apply the ointment and bandages to keep them clean until they heal."

Becca stares at the floor with a blank expression before slowly raising her head to look at Dr. Koleman.

"Becca, do you remember what happened?" he asks.

She noticeably swallows before answering, "Yes."

"Would you mind sharing what you remember?" The room is so fucking quiet I can hear every breath, every small squeak from her shifting on the bed.

"It doesn't matter. The past is the past for a reason, and it can stay there. I will continue to move forward." What the fuck? Is that a public relations response?

"Becca, your blood pressure is very high. Are you currently on any medications?" She blinks slowly before answering with a nod. "I need to know what they are."

"I'm on Valium," she answers while her fingers intertwine and pull on one another. Her eyes flash to me before finding the ground.

"Anything else?"

She bites the inside of her cheek and says, "The morning-after pill." I cock a brow at that answer, and then she continues, "Klonopin as well." She twists the sheets in her hand. "Just at night though. The Klonopin helps me sleep."

"How long have you been on these?"

"Almost three months. I was hoping to wean off of them, but it didn't go well," she answers with a hint of trepidation.

"What happened when your doctor lowered the dose?"

"Just an anxiety attack." She says it casually, like it doesn't even matter. "It's been working very well."

"I can see that. Your blood pressure is very high at the moment though, Becca."

"I see." Her words are sharp.

He leans forward and speaks with gravity in his voice. "I'm worried that you may be in a bit of shock."

"And what can I do to fix that?" She looks expectantly at

him, and I can't fucking believe it.

"We'll know more tomorrow. I'd like you to take your pills if you have them on you."

Her eyes find mine as she answers with a bit of irritation, "They're at my home."

"No need to worry. I'll be back soon with new medication."

"No need. I need to go home to get a few things." She starts to stand, and I move directly in her path.

"I'll get everything you and Jax need; you aren't going home."

Her eyes flash with anger. "I think you've done enough." Her words are designed to hurt me, and they're effective, but I ignore them.

"You would really put Jax in danger?" That gets her attention. She clenches her jaw.

"What am I supposed to do then? Nothing? Just let life roll over me?" Her breathing picks up as her voice gets louder. "Just lie there and let life fuck me over time and time again?" Her hands shove against my chest, surprising me, but I stand still and hardly budge. "What do you want from me?!" Tears burn in her eyes as she waits for a response, keeping her gaze firmly on mine.

This is the emotion I expected. More anger than I thought. But this is more of what I had anticipated.

"You just need to come with me, and I'll take care of everything."

A humorless laugh slips past her lips. "No you won't."

She doesn't say these words with anger. They're simply stated as fact. "No one's going to take care of me except for me. And I take care of Jax," she says as she sidesteps me and mumbles under her breath, "no one else."

She opens the door barely an inch before my palm slams on it and closes her in.

"You need to relax for just a minute and think things through, Becca. You don't really have any options."

She shakes her head and tries to pull the door open, even though she can clearly see I'm pushing against it. "I'll just go to the police; they'll be able to do something."

My blood freezes, and I stare hard at the doctor. She's still trying to open the door, completely unaware of what she just said and what it means to say those words.

I gentle my hand on her back and lean in close to whisper. "I'm going to pretend you didn't say that. But those words better never come out of your mouth again."

Her hand falls from the door, and her eyes go round. She turns quickly, shaking her head. "That's not what I meant." She swallows and puts her hands on my chest, still frantically shaking her head. "That's not what I meant." Her breaths come in short pants and she repeats herself for a third time. "That's not what I meant."

I rub my hand on her back in soothing circles, shushing her. "I didn't hear what you said, doll." I place a soft kiss on her forehead. "What was it you said you were going to do?" I give her a hard look with narrow eyes, and fucking hate myself for it. She needs comfort right now, but she keeps pushing me away. I'll do what I have to do to make this right, even if that means being a prick right now.

A frown mars her face, and sadness clouds her eyes with defeat. "I said I'll do as you say, Dom." Her voice is small as she pulls her hands away from my chest.

"Good girl. I'll take care of you." She swallows thickly and doesn't look at me. Doesn't answer me.

Becca's a strong woman. I knew that the day she stepped into my office, but she doesn't have to be right now. She can't be strong all the time. It's not possible. Right now she needs someone to lean on, someone to take the lead. Her small hands are still on my chest as I pull her into me. She's resistant and stubborn. I smile and kiss her hair. She's gonna have to learn to let me take care of her. I'm not gonna give her any other option.

CHAPTER 13

DOM

Becca looks back at herself in the mirror with hollow eyes. I watch her pupils shrink and focus on every tiny mark on her face. Every bruise. She looks beat to hell, because she was. Looking at the marks makes my blood boil. I can't wait to get my hand wrapped around their throats so I can beat them to bloody pulps.

"I'm going to need better concealer," she says with no emotion whatsoever. Her fingertips gently touch her face. She's tracing a cut over her eye and hovering over a large bruise on her jaw.

"I'll get you everything that you need."

"We could just make a stop at my house for most of the things I need."

I shake my head and don't wait for her to continue her thought as I say, "I sent Clara out a bit ago to get you new things." Her eyes dart to mine in the mirror.

That's very kind, but I don't need-"

"It's not about need. It's about you pleasing me. I seem to recall you saying you'd do what I asked?"

Her face falls, and I feel like a prick. But she fucking needs this. She won't let me in any other way.

"I wanna see Jax."

"You should shower first," I say and as soon as the words are out of my mouth, I wish I could shove them back in. Who am I to keep her away from him? He's her son. But she really looks like hell. I can only imagine how he'd react seeing his mom all beat up. "If you wanna-"

"You're right. I'll shower first." She turns around with her back to me and looks at the shower. It's nothing like what I have at home. I have a state of the art shower system with rainforest shower heads and a solid bench to relax on with the steam going. It also happens to be good for fucking, too. But we're not at my house yet. I wanna get her put together before she sees Jax, and he's staying with Ma till then. So instead she's gonna have to settle for a simple tub and shower setup with a plain white curtain. I mean, it'll do the trick, but it's not going to feel nearly as nice, especially on her sore muscles.

"I have a steam room at my house. Just clean up here, and you can relax tonight."

She turns her head slowly to look at me. I wish she'd fucking talk to me. A tight smile pulls at my lips. Really though, how much has she said to me since I've met her? Nothing, really. She's barely said anything to me. Other than her texts on why we shouldn't be fucking. I may have looked her up and practically stalked her, but she doesn't know much about me at all. And I was just doing what I needed to so I could get her in bed.

It's painfully obvious that I don't know this woman. I almost got her killed, and I don't even know her. And she sure as hell doesn't know me.

"Go ahead and hop in, doll. I'll sit here and keep you company." I try to lighten my tone.

She slips off the baggy shirt I put her in and pulls back the curtain with one hand while covering her body with the other. My eyes linger on every bruise, the bandages around her wrists and ankles.

I need to get my mind off this shit. I take a seat on the bench by the towel rack and sit back with my ankles crossed.

"Remember the bandages-" I start, but she doesn't let me finish.

"I know. I'll leave them on until I get out." A moment passes in silence.

"You like sports, doll?" It's my go-to conversation starter.

For all occasions. It's something I know enough about to dominate the conversation, so I just run with it.

"I was raised a Dolphins fan, so I'm used to hating football by now." Her sarcastic answer isn't what I expected. I chuckle and grin with my eyes on her vague silhouette behind the curtain.

"Dolphins? How the hell did that happen?" I ask with the smile still on my face. It's a rare day when I suggest betting on Miami. But if that's what she likes, so be it.

"My dad liked them. I liked dolphins. It was an easy choice. I mean, they're like the only team to go into the Super Bowl undefeated, right?"

I huff a laugh. "That was like two decades ago."

"Still counts." Her upbeat reply makes me grin. "I like watching the games. I used to go out to a bar and watch them every Sunday. Beer, pizza, wings. You know the way it is. It's a nice escape."

"Used to?"

"Life got busy." She answers with less enthusiasm, making me wish I'd prompted a different question, like who she used to go with. But I know she met her husband in college, so I can guess that answer, and I don't like it.

I smirk at the curtain. "So you know something about football?"

"I know a little. Like I know the game. I just don't know the players."

"What about other sports?"

Her voice noticeably changes. More engaging, more excited. "Jax plays soccer."

"Isn't he three?"

"Well, you know, he likes to kick the ball on the field."

"So your little man is an athlete?" I ask her, but she's quiet. Her hands have fallen to her sides. It's silent for a moment; the water spray is the only noise I can hear. And then I watch as her hands move to her face, and a sob comes from the shower.

"Doll, you alright?" My stomach drops. I wonder if it's finally catching up to her now. If she's going into shock like Doctor Koleman was worried about.

"Dom?" she finally asks. Her words are muted by the flow of the water. "If something happens to me, please don't take it out on my son." My heart clenches, and my vision blurs. The smile vanishes off my face. "I have money. I'll do anything-"

"Stop it, Becca. Nothing's happening to you." I'm hard with my response, but I don't fucking like the way she's talking.

"I'm not stupid, Dom." Her sad voice carries a heavy weight. "Please just don't hurt him." I have to take a deep breath and cover my face with my hands. She thinks I'm gonna hurt her son? I can't fucking believe it. "We don't have family, but I have a friend in Texas." Her voice is tight and full of tension. "It's been a while, but-"

"Doll. I'm gonna need you to knock it the fuck off before I lose my self-control." That at least gets her to shut up. "I'm not gonna hurt you, or your son."

"You're just going to let me go?"

No. My internal answer is immediate, but I don't voice that. I don't know what I want from her. I know I feel like shit about what happened, and that I want to make it right. But that's all I know for certain. "You can't go until we have De Luca."

"Is that who took me?" she asks with a hesitant voice. We don't talk business with women. They stay out of it. Always. I don't know what to tell her. She's just standing still in the shower. The water's going to get cold fast if she doesn't hurry her ass up.

"Doll, wash up." After a moment, she reaches for the body wash. I want her to be at ease; I want her to relax. Letting women know about the business isn't a smart thing to do. But then again, she's involved already. "De Luca's a dead man for what he did to you. I promise you that."

Chapter 14

Becca

I let my eyes close for a moment, just feeling the heat on my skin. Calming, relaxing. I focus on the positive. I breathe in deep and slow. It makes my chest hurt, but I ignore it. My entire body feels like it's throbbing. The bandages around my ankles and wrists are soaked, and the heat stings my wounds.

Focus on the positive. We're safe. My eyes pop open. That's a lie. I'm not safe, and I haven't the faintest clue if Jax is safe right now. My son is downstairs, *supposedly*. If I don't do what Dom wants, I have no reassurance that Jax will be alright. Tears slip from the corners of my eyes. I'm at the mercy of the mob. I need to get us out of here. I need to get away. I can't believe I let this happen to Jax. I've dragged him into this by being careless. By recklessly falling for Dom, for his touch.

Something deep inside me is soothing my worry, telling me it's alright. Wanting me to believe everything will work out, and that Dom is telling the truth. But I've listened to that voice before, and I've been fooled. I refuse to listen to it now.

I should've called the cops the moment Dom showed up on my doorstep. Instead, I was foolish. Again. I lose all sense of judgment when he looks at me with those sharp lust-filled eyes. But I can't afford to be weak. Especially not now. I just need a moment to figure something out. There has to be a way out of this. But my mind is blank. They'll kill me if I run. Either the assholes who fucked me up before, or Dom and his mob.

My heart won't stop racing. It's trying to beat out of my chest or climb up my throat. My body shudders, and I realize the water isn't quite as hot. It doesn't feel relaxing anymore.

"De Luca's a dead man for what he did to you. I promise you that." I hear the threat in Dom's voice, and it chills me to the bone. I know he saved me, but at what cost? What does he want from me? A shiver runs through my body. I know exactly what he wants. But for how long? How long will that keep me safe?

I hear a faint knock at the bathroom door, and it makes my entire body jump. My blood is coursing with adrenaline, my heart's racing, and I'm struggling to breathe. I need my medicine.

No, I don't! I can do this. I've done it before. I can get through this. I lean against the tiled wall and try to keep myself from having another panic attack.

"I'll be right back, doll."

Dom's confident voice and use of that little pet name makes my body calm. A sense of ease and peace flows through me. I hold onto that for as long as I can. The door opens and a small gust of chill goes through the room, but then it's gone. I wait for him to speak. I wait for something. But he doesn't say anything. I stay in the shower for as long as I can. Until the water has lost nearly all of its heat.

The faucet turns off with a screech, and I peek my head out from behind the curtain.

The room is empty, save a small bit of steam clouding the mirror. He left a fresh towel for me on the bench. I walk out of the stall and quickly wrap it around my body. The bandage on my right wrist is falling. So I slowly and gently unwrap it. And then the rest.

My chest hardens as I look at my body. Quick flashes of memory appear before my eyes and I fold into myself, crumpling onto the floor and bite down the scream threatening to hurl itself from my mouth. A cold sweat forms on my body, and my hands start to shake. My body trembles and rocks. I lie against the tile floor, needing to cool down and focus on my breathing. It's black. Everything is black. But I can hear them. I think I know what they look like. I see his fist coming for me, and a small whimper escapes.

No!

I will not let this hurt me. I have to be strong. I push it down. I push everything away. It's only a memory. It's only a memory. So many times I've had to remind myself.

This isn't the first time I've been hurt, and this will not break me. I won't let them. I grind my teeth and will the anxiety down. Just as the calmness washes through me, I remember the crash. I see the large oak tree. I hear the screeching tires, my mother screaming. I see my father's arms fly out. One in front of his face, the other to the passenger seat.

My eyes fly open, and I force myself to sit upright. I will not go back. I will not go back there. It won't be of any use. I should know. Giving into fears and false hopes only makes the pain grow.

I stand up and walk to the sink and countertop. The ointments are waiting for me along with a few Q-tips, courtesy of Dom. At least he seems to be taking care of me. I'll feel better once he lets me see Jax. I feel hopeless knowing he has the ability to keep Jax away from me right now. He has control over me. I'm not sure he means to use it like that. But it doesn't change the fact it's true. I can't disobey him and risk my son.

A chill goes through my bones, remembering how I said I'd go to the cops. I bend down and gently rub more ointment into the cuts on my ankles. They're an angry red. Anger is appropriate. I'm angry at myself for being so stupid.

Stupid to say that to a man who holds so much power

over me, and power in general. And stupid to be reliving the past. It's been years since I've remembered that night. The night my entire world changed, and the only family I had died. I look down at my wrists and examine the scratches and raw open cuts. This is nothing. This will heal.

Shards of glass cut deeper than rope, and that healed. A sickness grows in my gut; it's not the physical pain that causes the terrors and anxiety. It's the memory of when the pain happened. I won't let them haunt me. I can't. I can't go back to being useless, all at the mercy of a memory.

An image of the tattoo flashes before my eyes. A bright green dragon and a red shield. It's burned into my memory. That memory, that one I will remember. I won't forget the men. But I won't let them continue to hurt me. They may have tortured me and left me to die. But I won't give them any more of me. I close my eyes and remember Dom's promise. I nod my head.

They need to die.

CHAPTER 15

BECCA

"What's all this?" Dom's bed is covered with bags. I hold the towel close to my body. He's seen me before, but it's different now. I feel really fucking uncomfortable with his eyes on me.

"I was going to put it all in the car, but you should take a look at it first." He runs a hand through his hair. "I don't really know what you like."

"All this is for me?" What the hell?

"And Jax."

"This isn't necessary." I shake my head in disbelief. Everything I need is at home.

"I don't want you going back to your house." His voice is

hard and unmoving.

"I don't understand."

"Doll," he says and walks to me and places a hand on my chin. It takes everything in me not to pull away from him. "You need to learn to not ask questions. Alright?" Fuck that! Who doesn't ask questions? Although I don't open my mouth, he must read exactly what I'm thinking all over my face. I'm not all that good about being subtle with my emotions.

"We're having a few ex-SEALs check out your house and set up some surveillance."

"What the fuck for?" I almost rip the towel off my body, throwing my hands in the air. "I don't want strangers in my house. I don't want this!" I scream and give him a vicious look. I was perfectly okay before him. Everything was just fucking peachy before him.

"First off, I told you to stop asking questions." He grips my chin and stares into my eyes with a menacing look. "Second, you should really watch that smart mouth of yours." The heated look in his eyes as he scolds me sends a throbbing need to my clit. My anger instantly dissipates, replaced with desire. A very unhealthy amount of desire, considering the circumstances.

The way he controls me, commands me, makes me want to submit. My lips part, and my eyes soften as he leans down to mold his lips to mine. He pulls back and gentles his hand, moving it to the back of my neck.

"I got you into this, babe. I'm gonna get you out. I'll

make them pay and take care of you. *Both* of you." My heart stutters in my chest. I love that he thinks of my son. It's so easy to fall for this. For him. The thought snaps me out of the lust-filled haze.

His hand tightens on the nape of my neck and he says, "Uh-uh." His eyes narrow. "Don't you dare shut me out again." My eyes widen slightly. "Yeah, I know that look, doll." A cocky smirk pulls his lips up. He rests his head on my forehead. "You can't hide from me, Becca." His voice is low, but it's reassuring, not threatening.

It scares the fuck out of me.

"Can I see Jax now?" I ask in a timid voice I don't recognize. I clear my throat and square my shoulders. He's my son. And I want to see him now. It feels like it's been days since I've seen him. It's a feeling I don't like. I look around the room again for clothes. "I need to get dressed."

"Of course, doll." His fingertips lightly play along my jaw. "You wanna cover this up? Just so it doesn't scare the little guy?" I stare into his light blue eyes with a heavy heart. I wonder if that's on his mind because he's used to this kind of thing. Women covering up their bruises. The thought makes me turn away from him. I swallow thickly with my back to him, facing the bed.

"Did you happen to grab any makeup?" I ask quietly. It feels wrong to ask for things from him. But there are so many bags on the bed. I see a few names I recognize – Nordstrom,

Clinique, Gymboree, J. Crew. A Cartier bag catches my eye, and I inhale a sharp breath. You've got to be fucking kidding me. What would I need jewelry for? Surely that's not for me. And it sure as fuck isn't for Jax.

"Clara did. I gave her the black Amex, so I'm sure she just went crazy with it," he answers casually, and I just try to take it all in.

I pick up the Clinique bag and spot a few skincare items, but no makeup. I sift through the bags and underneath a La Perla bag with perfumed tissue paper is a bag with Lancome makeup. A shit ton of makeup. I pick it up along with the Clinique bag and take it to the bathroom.

"Take your time, doll." I give him a tight smile with my head down. I don't like this. I feel... cheap. At the same time, my lack of gratitude eats away at me.

"I'll pay you back for everything," I manage to get out as I turn the handle to the en suite.

"You can afford all that?" he asks, his voice laced with disbelief. I look at the bed and try to take it all in. Yeah, I guess if I sold my restaurant today. Maybe. I bite the inside of my cheek. "You're not paying me back, Becca."

I let his words sink in. They dig at my pride. I don't need his help. Fuck. Yes I do. I have to accept that. But I wish I didn't.

I'm covered from head to toe. A cream, boatneck cashmere sweater covers my wrists and the bruises on my arms. Dark burgundy yoga pants and a pair of comfy socks cover everything from my hips down. I don't think I've ever worn such luxurious clothing. It *looks* the same as some clothing I have and it's definitely my style, but it *feels* like heaven.

I haven't met Clara yet, but I like her. Or at least her taste in clothes. Although the scrap of material she calls underwear is not my taste. It's cute though. Lacy and delicate. Dom would shred it easily. My thighs clench thinking of him ripping through it and taking me again. I bite my bottom lip and scold myself. I know I'm trying to distract myself from everything that happened today, but that kind of behavior wouldn't be wise.

The doctor left Dom my pills. I took another codeine and a Valium and I'm not in much pain at all now, other than my ribs being a bit sore as I make my way down the stairs. I have to wince through the pain, but other than that, there's nothing. I feel too relaxed. I wish I hadn't taken the Valium; it makes me tired.

A small smile plays on my lips as I hear Jax laughing. We round the corner of the hall to a large open living room. And there he is, with a monster truck in hand, standing on the back of the sofa, about to push it down a ramp of cushions. It warms my heart all the way down to my toes. My little man. Relief floods through me. Thank God.

In that moment I feel so much gratitude for Dom. Emotions well up in my chest, and I push them away. My hand reaches for Dom's, and I squeeze. I don't know why. But it's all I can do. He gives my hand a squeeze back and looks at me with curiosity.

I know I'm in this shit because of him. I'm painfully aware of how fucking stupid I was. And even more so of how Rick is why I'm in this shit in the first place. But he didn't have to help me. He didn't have to make sure Jax was safe. He didn't have to come rescue me. I can't fucking help the tears running down my face. It's just too much for me to handle. Too much for me to accept. I push my back against the wall and try to calm myself. Jax is just around the corner, after all; I don't want him to see me like this.

"You alright, doll?" Dom brushes my tears away with his thumb. He looks like he doesn't know what to do. And that makes me laugh. I must look fucking crazy. Crying out of nowhere and then laughing at him. Maybe I am crazy at this point. Maybe this was all I could take. Judging by the look on Dom's face, he may be thinking I've lost it, too.

"I'm okay. I could be better, but I'm okay," I finally answer. I wipe my tears and look down at my fingers to make sure I haven't fucked up the concealer. Nothing. They're clean. This is some good shit to be able to withstand tears.

I push myself off the wall, and to my surprise, Dom wraps his arm around my waist and pulls me into him. His embrace is warm and comforting. I shouldn't like it so much. He's practically a stranger and definitely a dangerous man. I lean into him knowing all of that. I just need it.

As soon as I round the corner and Jax catches a glimpse of me, I kneel down and open my arms for him.

"Mommy!" he yells out, dropping the truck and running to me. It hurts when he slams into my chest, but I don't care. It feels so good just to hold him. I kiss his forehead and just hold him until he starts to push me away.

"Do you see trucks?" He runs back over to the pile of cushions and collects a truck to hold it up for me to see. "So big, mommy!" I can't speak; just looking at him has me too emotional to function, so I nod my head and make sure I'm smiling.

There's another little boy jumping on the cushionless sofa with an olive complexion with dark brown eyes and a faux Mohawk. He's grinning from ear to ear like he can hardly stand the anticipation of the drop.

"That's Gino," Dom huffs a small laugh at the little boy.

"Is he your nephew?" I ask.

"Basically." I think that's all I'm going to get, but then he continues. "Jimmy's my cousin, but we grew up together. We're all close." I nod as though I understand, but I don't. I don't know what that's like. "You'll meet him tonight. Clara's gone already, and Vince only comes home for Saturday and Sunday dinners."

An older woman, maybe in her fifties, walks into the

room from the kitchen. Her dark black hair with grey streaks is pulled into a chignon bun. Trailing her is the sweet smell of white wine and shrimp. I can only imagine she's cooking up shrimp scampi or something else that smells just as good. My mouth waters as I lick my lips.

"Hi, Becca. I'm Linda, Dom's Ma." She wipes her hands on a small kitchen towel and walks over to us on the other side of the room. I expect a handshake, but instead I'm greeted with a gentle hug. She looks over my face with a sad smile. "Would you like anything to drink?" It's not the question I anticipate. But then I remember Dom's warning about not asking questions.

I gently shake my head and reply, "I'm fine, thank you."

"You say that a lot, you know?" He looks down at me with a quizzical look on his face.

Linda interrupts our moment. "Shrimp scampi for dinner, it's almost ready." *I knew it!* She says the last bit with a teasing tone. We have shrimp scampi at my bistro. It's one of my favorite dishes. The reminder of the restaurant makes my gut sink. Dom still has my phone.

"I need my phone." I'm blunt, and I hope he doesn't push me on this. I have a PA that theoretically could handle everything, but in reality she constantly relies on me.

"Who are you going to call?" At first I'm pissed off at his question. and then I see the threat in his eyes. *The cops.*

"Not calling anyone; I just want to check on my business."

He reaches into his pocket and holds it out for me. As I reach for it, he pulls back.

"Kiss first." He turns his cheek to me. I roll my eyes, but stand on my tiptoes and plant a kiss on his cheek. For some reason his playfulness makes me feel lighter. And then I look at the phone and see all the messages. Four missed calls and thirty-two unread messages. Fuck. I sigh heavily and start with the texts, but the bottom one catches my eyes.

All taken care of. No worries. Just feel better!

I stare at the screen with confusion until Dom answers my unspoken question.

"I texted her and told her you'd be out of commission for a bit and gave her the number of our manager in case she needed help."

"Thank you." I can't imagine it's that easy though. I read through the messages, searching for anything indicating she still needs help. Nothing. She did everything without me today.

He holds out his hand for the phone back.

I purse my lips. "I don't like that."

He leans in close to answer, "After what you said upstairs, I'm nervous that you're going to do something stupid."

I shake my head and insist, "I won't. I don't know why I said it."

"I do," he says while taking my phone and putting it back in his pocket.

"What the hell does that mean?" *I do.* Like he knows

me like that.

"I told you to watch that tone, doll. I'm trying to go easy on you, but you can only push so much." The threat in his voice does all the wrong things to me. So I simply turn away from him and focus on the two little men playing with their toys who are completely unaware of what's happened today.

Dinner has been... telling. Jax is happy and playing with Gino. The men, Jimmy, Dom, and Dom's father Dante, have been joking and carrying on and playing with the kids. Even Linda's been poking fun at her husband. It's almost like today never happened. Like they weren't at a shootout. I'm not sure it's perfectly healthy, but I like it. I appreciate it. I don't want to wallow. I want to move on as quickly as possible.

I lean back slightly in the chair and lick the last bit of white wine butter sauce from my fingers. Linda knows how to cook, that's for damn sure. I've been quiet all dinner except for the dozen times I've commented on her food. Jax likes it too, which makes me happy since he hardly ever actually eats anything. I swear he lives off fruit snacks and apple juice.

Dom puts his hand on my thigh and squeezes. A sense of family and belonging that I haven't felt in so long overwhelms me. I watch him as he smiles and makes a face at Gino. Is this what it would be like, if what was between us was more?

Is that even an option? I never gave it a thought. Never considered it. A man like him doesn't settle down. But this feels so right.

No, what am I thinking? I could've died today because of him. A lump grows in my throat as I look at Jax smiling and bumping shoulders with Gino. I could never let this happen. As soon as Dom gives me the chance to leave, I'm going to take it. I can't allow Jax to grow up like this. Not with mobsters.

The lump grows thicker, threatening to choke me so I reach for my glass and try to calm myself.

"You look a little shaken." A sweet, low whisper of concern comes from my left.

I give Dom's mother a tight smile and say, "I'm fine."

Dom looks at me from the corner of his eyes with a frown and runs his hand down my thigh.

"I know I shouldn't ask, but if you'd like to talk, I'm here for you." I half expect the room to go silent, but Dom and the guys continue to joke and talk in the background. It's almost like white noise. Linda's light blue eyes are the same color as Dom's and they draw me in, offering me a place to confide.

"I don't know how you do it."

"Do what, dear?"

"This." I barely speak the word. *I don't know how you can be married to the mob.* I can't just come out and say that, but after a short moment she seems to understand.

"Some days, I don't either. But I love my family. We're

all good people." I stare at her as she takes another bite of shrimp. Are they? I highly doubt it, but then again I know nothing about it. I chance a question.

"What do they do?" I ask her with a low voice. The men continue their conversation, and a bellow of laughs surrounds me.

"What do you mean?" She tilts her head in confusion.

"I mean, like, what is it that they *do*?"

Her eyes widen, and her eyebrows raise. "Well, now. I don't ask those kinds of questions, and neither should you. *But*, I do happen to know that the bistro pulls in a hefty amount of money." I stare at her, considering her words. She can't possibly believe that owning the bistro is all they do. Drugs and guns and murder. That's what the mob does.

"When you love someone, it's amazing what you'd do for them." She gives me a warm smile and says, "One day I'll have to tell you how Dante and I met. I'm sure you haven't heard a story like ours before." Her blue eyes twinkle with happiness. "I love my family."

I consider her words. There's no doubt she does. There's obvious warmth and love in the room. But I could never raise my son like this. I feel like an asshole for judging her. And a hypocrite for fucking Dom and feeling so much for him so quickly. But this could never be my reality. Jax deserves a better chance at life. A good life. Not a life in the mob. This is temporary. I have to make sure this doesn't last.

CHAPTER 16

DOM

I thought things were going well. And then she started talking to Ma. Her little boy is in the back, so I'm not going to question her on the drive back to my house, but as soon as we get alone, I wanna know what's gotten into her head.

She looks so beautiful, leaning her head against the car door, sleeping. So peaceful. Peaceful is the right word. She's got faint wrinkles around her eyes, and I know it's from her stressing out. She's a type A personality without a doubt. I am too, but I don't let it run me into the ground like she does.

But then again, I didn't have the shitty luck she's been having. It's hard to believe a man would cheat on her. If I had to guess why, my guess would be money. His business had just failed. That, and she was making more than him. Maybe he felt emasculated. I don't know, and I don't really give a shit why. He was a fucking idiot for cheating on her. And for leaving her.

I turn the wheel up the drive and park in the garage as usual. It feels different though. I take a peek over my shoulder, and her little boy is passed out just like her. I don't want to wake either of them, so I silently slip out of my seat and gently close the door. I go around to Jax's door and carefully pull him out, letting his head rest on my shoulder. It's odd carrying a sleeping child. He's light and limp. Probably drooling on my shirt. I stifle my chuckle and carry him into the house.

I have a guest room upstairs that'll be perfect for him. It's right next door to my room, so I'm sure we'll hear him if he wakes up. I lay him down nice and gentle, and hold my breath while he readjusts and snuggles into the mattress. I really don't need this kid waking up and freaking out.

I turn around, and Becca nearly scares the shit out of me. My heart tries to jump up my fucking throat, and my blood shoots up with adrenaline. She's standing there, rubbing her eyes in the doorway. I'm happy she has them closed too, because my first instinct was to reach for my gun. I tuck it back into the holster and casually walk toward her like she didn't almost give me a heart attack.

"Bedtime, doll." I wrap my arm around her waist and pull her out of the room, but she resists me. I look down at her wide, frightened eyes with a confused look.

"I don't want to leave him alone." Oh, fuck that. She's sleeping with me. He sleeps alone at her place; he'll be fine here.

"He's already passed out, doll." I tug on her waist again. She takes a look at him and then back to me before pulling away from me. She strolls over to him, and I wait in the doorway. I hold back on everything until I know for sure what she's doing.

She leans over him and pets his hair before giving him a small kiss on the forehead. "Good night, my baby boy; I love you." I just barely hear her.

She rises slowly, not taking her eyes off of him before coming back to my side. "Good girl."

As soon as we get to the bedroom, she looks around like she's lost. Like she's a nervous virgin. I like that she's a bit frightened. I like that I can take her control away. She'll learn to love it. I'll show her how good it can be when someone else is in charge.

I stroll to my dresser and grab a white tee shirt for her to wear for the night. I should go downstairs and grab all her shit. But I don't feel like it, and she'll look good in my shirt anyway. It's that, or she can go naked. I'm fine either way. When I look up to toss her the shirt, she's standing by the nightstand, digging through her purse.

"Whatcha looking for, doll?" I ask, walking up behind her.

"My pills." Her answer makes my body go cold. I don't like that she takes medication. I understand she's wound tight and going through some shit, but I don't like it. She grabs a bottle and pops the lid.

"Which one is that?" It wasn't my business before, but now she's in my care, so I want to know everything.

"Codeine," she says while palming a single pill.

Shit, I feel like an asshole for thinking like that. Like she shouldn't be taking medicine. Given what she's been through, it's amazing she's doing everything that she is.

"I'll get you a glass of water, babe." I jog down the stairs so I can get back to her quickly. Guilt weighs down on my shoulders. She wouldn't be in pain if it wasn't for me.

When I get back to her she's sitting on the bed, looking down at her bare feet and wearing the shirt I gave her. She has a sad look on her face. I can't even begin to guess what's causing it. There's so much shit she has to deal with.

She takes the glass with a grateful smile and quickly swallows the pain meds.

I sit on the bed next to her and take a deep breath. I've been holding off on talking. It's what we do in the family. You don't talk about shit. It's done and over with, and you move on. And we sure as shit don't discuss any business in front of women. But this is different. She's involved. She's hurt. I need to understand what's going on in her head in order to help her.

"Tell me what hurts, doll?" I start with an easy question.

She gives me a weak smile and says, "I'm f-" She stops her

word and bites her bottom lip while smiling.

"You think that's funny?" I shake my head. It's a little funny that she always says she's fine, but not really. 'Cause she's not fine.

"I'm alright, Dom." I turn my body toward her and run my finger over the small bruise showing through her makeup.

"Take all this off so I can look at you." I know she's roughed up. And that there's more to her injuries than just the physical component. I'm gonna start with the bruises, then work my way to everything else.

She stares back at me for a minute with a blank look, like the one she gave me earlier and for a second I think I'm gonna have to remind her that she needs to listen to me. She swallows and gets up, heading for the open bathroom door to my en suite. I follow a few steps behind her. I'll set her up with the steam room as soon as I get a good look at her. It'll help her muscles. I should know. I've gotten the shit kicked out of me a few times, and the steam always helps relieve the soreness.

I hear her gasp when she turns on the light, and that makes me smile. My place is pretty fucking sweet. I didn't hold back on the upgrades. Her bare feet make a soft padding noise as she walks across the travertine floor to the floating marble vanity. The sink itself is carved out of the marble, and I can tell she's impressed. She turns to take in the rest of the room. The river rock shower takes up the back half of the room, with glass doors that separate it from the rest of the bathroom. There's a comfortable bench inside where she can lounge while the steam goes to work on her body. In the center of the room is a rustic bowl soaking tub also made of stone. She walks slowly to it and runs her hand along the dark grey edge.

"You wanna soak a bit, doll?" She startles when my low voice seems to echo off the walls of the large bathroom. She looks at me with wide eyes, and then stares at the tiled floor. "I thought you might wanna lie down in the steam room, but a soak in the tub would be nice, too." I still have some of that sea salt for healing. Not the shit that stings, but the good stuff. I take a step toward her, and she takes a step back.

"What's gotten into you, doll?" She's wearing that same guarded expression from dinner. I don't fucking like it.

"How..." She struggles to ask whatever's on her mind. Whatever her question is, it can't be good. There's a reason we don't like the women asking questions. We don't want them involved in this shit, it makes them targets. There's usually an understanding about this. Women stay out of it.

But that's not how shit worked out for her. She can't just go along with things and leave the business to the men.

"Ask it, doll; whatever you want to know. I'll tell you right now." That's partially a lie. I know it, but I don't want to tell her there's shit I'm not going to answer. I'll let her ask whatever's on her mind. Hopefully it's nothing too specific. Something I can talk around.

"How many people have you killed?" she asks in a voice so low, it takes me a moment to actually understand her question.

Red fucking flags shoot up in my head. Cops ask questions like that. I run a hand through my hair and watch as her knuckles turn white gripping the edge of the tub. I need to get her ass in the tub first. It's not like she's a cop. She's not. Tony would've figured that out if she was. And she's not wearing a wire. Even if she was, I've got the blocker set up in every room of the house. No way a rat is getting shit out of me in my own home.

I take a step toward the tub, and she reacts with fear. Taking a sharp inhale, and another step away from me. She's scared to ask me questions, and I don't like that. I don't know how Pops does it. I don't know why Ma doesn't ask, and never has. But it sure as shit isn't because of fear.

I push the stopper down and lean over and turn the faucet on, letting the water warm before dipping my fingers into it. I turn the heat up a bit and walk to the shelves for the salt. It's pink. Maybe she'll like that. I scoop out a bit and drop it right below the running water and dip my fingers back in. That should be good for her. Maybe it'll help her relax some.

"Get in, babe. Relax a bit, and then we'll talk." I sit my ass on the edge of the tub and grip her hips, pulling her in between my legs. Her lips part, and her small hands brace herself on my chest. I pull her closer and gently kiss under her ear, on that tender spot below her neck and it works like a charm. She relaxes slightly, leaning into me. A soft sigh leaves her as I leave another open-mouth kiss on the crook of her neck.

I love that sound, the little moan of satisfaction. I want to push for more; I want to run my hands from her thighs up to her ass, and squeeze. My dick hardens thinking about fucking her against the tub. The tub is solid and I could pound into her and force her to take the intensity of each thrust. But there's no doubt it'd leave bruises. And she's so hurt already.

I pull away from her, remembering her current state and place a soft kiss against her lips. I take her hand in mine and gently unravel the bandages. She did a shit job of putting them on. I should've done it earlier. My thumb brushes lightly over the raw skin on her wrists. She struggled against them. The abrasions from the rope piss me off. A deep hurt settles in my chest, and it takes everything in me to keep my face from showing my anger.

They hurt her to get to me. They tried to kill her. And they wanted me to see.

As adrenaline pumps through my blood and my heartbeat picks up, her small hands land on my shoulders and rub soothing circles. A satisfied groan rumbles through me. My hands find the small of her back, and I rest my forehead against her chest. She's so warm and comforting. It takes a moment to notice that her arms have wrapped around me, and her head is resting on top of mine.

I tilt my head up and catch her bottom lip between my

teeth. I pull back slightly at her whimper before letting her go. Her half-hooded eyes stare back with a spark of lust.

My doll fucking loves it rough. Her thighs clench in between my legs. I want to fuck into that hot, tight cunt so fucking much. My dick roars back to life as her eyes stare into mine, waiting for me to take her. "You want me to fuck you, doll?" Her fingers touch her lips and her eyes stare at mine as she slowly nods her head once.

I want it too, but not right now. I need to get her to tell me what's going on in her head. I need answers. And so does she.

"Be a good girl and strip." I watch her body as she pulls the shirt above her head and lets it fall onto the floor. Her breasts are full and lush, and I lean forward and take a nipple into my mouth. Teasing me, teasing her. She gasps as I bite down and pull back. She has one hand on my head, and one on her other breast. Her fingers pinch and pull her hardened nipple while her other hand tries to push me closer to her. *Naughty girl.*

I let her nipple go and love how her mouth forms a perfect "O" and her eyes close in pleasure. "Bad girl. You don't direct this show, doll." I set a bad example the last time we fucked by letting her lead like that. But damn, it turned me on. My dick jumps, remembering how fucking good it was. My breathing is picking up, and my fingers are itching to play with her body. My eyes trail down her skin, and then I see the bruises.

"You need a salt soak." I have to keep my mind focused.

Her ass isn't topping from the bottom anymore. She just wants to fuck me. Other than that, she's scared of me. Which isn't necessarily a bad thing. But for some reason, I don't like it.

"Are you a fucking sadist?" She takes a step back and gives me a bewildered look. Well, she's obviously not that scared. I guess when her sweet cunt's begging for my attention she's not so afraid.

I smirk at her and push off the edge of the tub, putting my body right in front of hers. I let my lips barely brush up against hers and respond, "It's not gonna hurt." My hands grab her ass and I squeeze her cheeks before lifting her up. She wraps her legs around my body and lets her heat rub against the bulging erection covered by my sweats. "I promise I'll make it good for you." I rock my dick against her heat and smile when that small moan parts her lips again. I turn with her in my arms and slowly put her in the water. She tries to hold onto me for a moment, and her legs tighten around me as her ass hits the warm water.

"Be a good girl for me, doll. I don't want to have to spank that ass tonight." Her eyes shoot to mine and search my face, trying to figure out if that's an empty threat. She's such a kinky bitch.

She slowly unwraps her legs and hesitantly sinks her hand into the water. As soon as one leg's submerged, she drops her weight and relaxes, a look of pure bliss on her face. The steam from the bath rises around her. The salts leave a thin layer of translucent white on the surface of the water. Her breasts barely peek out just enough to tease me. Her nipples are hard, and they're begging me to suck them. But not right now. I have to keep reminding myself.

She leans her head back against the tub and looks at the open door to the bathroom, a slightly worried look on her face.

"What's distracting you, babe?" I sit on the edge of the tub, wiping the water from my arms onto my sweats. She tilts her head and narrows her eyes, wondering how I knew her mind had gone somewhere else. "You're very easy to read."

"Jax." Her answer spreads warmth through my chest.

"What about your little man?" A gentle smile plays at her lips for a moment before she sighs.

"I just want to check on him." She swallows and brings her hands out of the water to pull her hair from her shoulders and off of her face.

"I'll go." I start to get up. That's an easy thing to check. Just make sure the little dude's still knocked out. She sits straight up and grabs my hand with hers, stopping me.

I look back at her, wondering what the fuck that's about. She swallows thickly and looks between me and the door. "It's a new place, and he doesn't know you." She gives me an answer to my unspoken question.

"He'll be asleep." I hope he's fucking asleep. "Do kids get up throughout the night?" I thought that was like a *baby*, baby thing.

She shakes her head and answers, "No, not usually." Her eyes are still wide and they're pleading with me, but I'm not sure what it is that she wants. It's fucking hard figuring out this broad.

"Alright then, I'll be back in a sec." I pull my hand away and she lets me, settling back against the tub. "If he's up, I'll bring him in the bedroom for you."

She seems to relax a bit and says, "Thank you." But that look is still in her eyes. I don't like it. I'm not going to bed until I figure out what the fuck's going on with her.

CHAPTER 17

BECCA

"Passed the fuck out." Dom strolls into his bathroom like nothing's wrong and squats next to me by the tub.

I give him a forced smile as I say, "Good." I take a deep breath.

"What's bothering you, doll?" I look back at him like he's lost his damn mind. Am I taking crazy pills? I was kidnapped by a group of men who wanted and tried to kill me, and now I'm being held against my will with my son by a man that's no good for me.

My arms splash the water as they rise up and cross over my knees to pull them into my chest. The movement of the hot water on my wounds makes them sting slightly, but it's instantly relieved by the salts in the water. It feels so fucking good. "What are the plans, exactly?" I like order; I like plans. More than that, I like knowing where my life is going so I can direct things to an appropriate path. Right now I have none of that. I have no control. And I don't fucking like it. But I also don't have a choice.

"De Luca's a dead man."

I'm quick to answer, "He wasn't when he took me." Hearing that name makes my body cower in the water. I hate it. I hate that I can't control how much my body hurts thinking of what he's done to me.

He shifts on the edge of the tub. "I'm sorry for that. I really am, babe. But I'm gonna make sure he pays."

"Is he the one with the tattoo?" I close my eyes, remembering the vibrant green against his tanned skin.

"I thought you didn't see anything?" He leans closer to me with his eyes narrowed. As if he suspects I lied to him. I should be scared, but I'm not. Instead I'm pissed.

"Don't fucking look at me like that. When they took me, that's all I saw."

His hand shifts up to grip my chin. "That mouth of yours. I swear to God it's going to get you into trouble."

"Why'd he...?" I try to push the words out, but my teeth grind together and my body stiffens. I don't want to think about it. I don't want to go back to what happened.

"His dad used to be a big deal, but he got busted and

De Luca just got out of prison. He's playing fast and loose. Targeting the big guys, and being sloppy about it. He's only been out for a week, and there's already a target on his back. Him and the few people he has following him around will be dead by the end of the week. No one gets away with the shit he's pulling. Not in this business."

I pull my knees further into my chest. I want to ask him again. I want to know everything. But I keep reminding myself that curiosity killed the cat.

"Talk to me, doll," Dom says then gets up from his seat on the tub and walks behind me. I look over my shoulder as he gets something from the wooden shelf in the corner and then drags a bench from the stall over to the back of the tub. I turn and face the wall as his hands come down on my shoulders. *Massage oil.* It smells so good, like chamomile and some kind of citrus. His thumbs dig into my sore muscles. It reminds me how much my body hurts.

The punches I could take, but being hung up like that, fighting my restraints? My head hurts remembering how I smacked it over and over against the edge of the sink. But it worked. I saved myself. If I hadn't fought... My heart stills, and my body tenses. I force my body to relax and close my eyes. There's no reason to think like that.

"Ask me again, and I'll tell you. You just relax and talk to me." I don't believe him. He's not going to answer a damn thing.

I take a deep inhale as his hands work my shoulders and

then glide up my neck. Fuck, it feels so good. My head goes limp, and I struggle to think of a question. I remember asking him earlier and not getting an answer, so I settle on asking that one again. "How many men have you killed?"

"A lot. I can't tell you how many, doll." My eyes pop open at his confession and my shoulders go stiff, giving away my fear. "Relax, babe. They all knew it was coming; they all had a gun aimed at me, too."

"If I hadn't had the money, would you have killed me?" He huffs a laugh.

"First of all, dead men can't pay you. It does set a bad example letting people get away with not paying you, though. The first thing, the *smart* thing to do, is to not let a man make a bet he can't afford." His hands stop, and I hear him swallow before he continues. "I knew... your ex could pay. If he hadn't shown up with the money, then we would've had a problem."

"What kind of problem?" I have to ask; I need to know.

"I'd have drained his bank account." I look up at him in absolute shock. "Yeah, doll. I have my ways." He pushes my shoulders enough to get me facing the wall again, and his hands continue rubbing soothing circles over my body. "But that wouldn't be enough. I'd have to make an example of him."

"What..." I want to ask what he'd do specifically. I try to push it out, but I can't.

"What would I have done? Do you really wanna know, babe?" I hesitate to answer. "I would've hurt him really bad, but it would've ended with him. Johnny should've told you that when you answered your ex's text. His debt wasn't on you."

He places a small kiss on my neck and says, "Don't worry about it, doll. The money's already in your bank account."

His words shock me. My body splashes the water as I turn to face him. "For real?" I ask.

"Yeah, doll. You didn't owe me. You never did." A small smile pulls at my lips as I settle back against the tub.

A moment passes in silence while he continues to rub my sore body.

"What if I was the one who owed you?" I want to know.

"If you owed me and you couldn't pay?" he asks.

"What would you have done to me?" I ask to clarify and again his hands pause, but then they continue to rub along my back, moving deeper and lower. His breath tickles along my back.

"Doll, I would've never hurt you." He kisses the crook of my neck and I find myself relaxing into him, but I don't believe him.

For some reason, my lips open and the words tumble out, "I don't believe you. You would've hurt me."

He chuckles, and his hot breath on my neck sends shivers through my body, but heats my core. His arms dip into the water and wrap around my body. "What do you think I would've done to you, doll?" His hands run down my stomach and then lower, rubbing my hips and then massaging my upper thighs. My legs part, giving him access to my heat. My clit throbs for his touch. I'm so fucking hot for him. My chest rises as I breathe in deep and tilt my hips for him.

His hand cups my pussy as he asks, "You think I would've made you pay with this, babe?" His fingers play along the folds of my pussy and circle my clit.

My head falls back; my mind is consumed with the thought of him fucking me in his office. Taking me on the floor. Forcing me.

"Would you have liked that?" He lets out a deep, low and breathy laugh. "I know you fucking liked it when you paid that way for the interest. How many times do you think I'd have taken you for owing me that much?"

"Hmm." I can't answer. I just want him to keep touching me while I think about how he took me against the wall.

He laughs again and then moves forward to push a thick finger inside me. "You would've loved to pay your debt to me with your pussy."

His finger moves in and out of me, pushing against the front wall and forcing soft moans through my lips. A tingle grows through my body, making my legs tremble. "I don't do that though, babe. I don't make bets with women." He adds another finger and rubs along that hot bundle of nerves, sending a radiating fire spreading through my trembling limbs. "I don't take pussy as payment." I hardly hear his words as my back bows, and he pushes against my clit with his thumb.

"Only you; I couldn't resist that temptation." His words

set me off, and my orgasm rips through me. His fingers continue to pump in and out of me roughly. He fucks me without mercy as my thighs close tightly around him, and my body twists. His other arm wraps around my chest, holding my body still while l thrash with my release riding through my body in waves. He draws my orgasm out, forcing me to take it. As l scream out my pleasure his lips cover mine, sealing my moans in our kiss.

My body settles as the aftershocks slow. He slips his fingers out of me, and l miss his touch immediately. He gently places me back against the tub and leaves me to lie limp in the warm water. My eyes close, and l nearly fall asleep. I'm so relaxed and exhausted.

His arms wrap around me, one under my bent knees and the other behind my back as he lifts me out of the water. He dries my body off, and l make a weak attempt to help. He pushes my hands away and continues patting my body dry, then leaves the towel on the ground to carry me to the bedroom. l try to sit in his arms, but he whispers in my ear, his voice a little more than a murmur, "l got you, doll." With his breath on my neck and his lips placing gentle kisses on my neck, he lays me on the bed and l drift off to sleep.

CHAPTER 18

BECCA

My body falls forward. But it can't. I need to go forward; I need to block the punch that's coming, but I can't. I'm held back. My face slams against something hard, forcing my neck to whip to the side and sending a jolt of pain through my body. It hurts. It all hurts. My body is sore and my wrists and ankles are rubbed raw. It hurts so fucking much.

Slap! A hard smack to my face from the other side shoots a throbbing pain across my face. I try to move my arms, but they're tied. Ugh! I try to lean forward after another punch to my stomach. The air leaves my lungs, and my chest tightens with pain. I'm pinned by hands. Pinned back by restraints... the belt.

I'm pinned back by the seat belt. The tires screech. The car crashes forward. My body jolts forward. The metal twists and groans. The glass shatters. My mom screams. I can't see her. Only my dad. My vision focuses on the tree. Heat overwhelms my shaking body. And then nothing.

No sound. Shards of glass stick out of my trembling arm. I carefully lift it and grasp the broken glass. My shaking fingers slip, and the pain makes me moan in agony. My voice. It's the only noise. I try to move; I need to help them...

"Becca!" Who's screaming my name? They can't. They can't yell for me. "Wake up!" They never yelled for me. "Babe, wake up!" My body shakes, and I struggle to move.

My eyes slowly open. "Becca?" Dom's face is pained; his light blue eyes look so sad. I blink back the tiredness overwhelming me, and that's when I feel the pain.

"Dom." I wince. Fuck, my body hurts.

"Shit." He lays me down on the bed and crawls to the nightstand. He leans over, still on the bed and reads the back of the bottle. Yes, please. My chest fucking hurts, and these damn abrasions on my ankles and wrists sting like a bitch. I want to climb back into the bath.

"Thank you," I manage to say before opening my mouth to take the pill. He tilts the glass of water to my lips and I take it with a trembling hand. Fuck, it hurts.

"Are you alright?" he asks with a wary look. His brows are pinched together, making a deep crease in his forehead.

"I'm fine," I answer, handing the glass back.

He takes the glass and sets it on the table. "I fucking hate that you do that," he says, crawling back to lie next to me. He pulls my body into his gently. "You're not fine." He kisses my neck. "You weren't fine."

I have a vague memory of being in pain before waking up in his arms. "I still hurt, but it will take some time to heal."

"That's not what I'm talking about." His voice is hard.

"I don't understand."

"You were begging for it to stop." His voice is pained. I turn in his arms and watch as he pinches the bridge of his nose. "You kept saying 'no'." I turn back on my side with my back to his chest and stare across the room.

"It was just a dream." It's the only answer I have for him.

"It was a memory."

"What do you want from me?" I ask him with contempt. His grip on me tightens.

"I just want you to talk to me." He pulls me into his chest and kisses my neck. His tender touch makes me relax.

"I don't know what you want me to say." What can I say? They hurt me. I'm still getting over it. There. What more can I offer?

"You can't just hide from this." His voice is just barely more than a murmur.

"It's not hiding; it's moving on. That's what you do. You move on."

"How can you move on without giving yourself any time to grieve?"

"You want me to be sad?" I turn in his arms and keep far enough away to look straight into his eyes. "Not everyone grieves the same way. Some people take time to really grasp the reality. Others seek out humor and positivity. Then there are people who'd rather just leave what can't be undone alone, and move forward with what they can change." I search his face for his reaction, but he gives me nothing.

"I can't change what happened to me. I'm only in charge of the present and my future. I learned that long ago. And I'm happy with that."

"How can you move on so quickly?" His voice is laced with disbelief.

"I haven't. Grief is a journey. It never ends." Shock sparks in his eyes, and then understanding. If there is an end, I have yet to find it.

"How bad does it hurt?"

"The medicine is already working." It is. My body already feels less tense, and the sharp pains have turned dull.

He shakes his head gently. "Not that pain." My chest hurts from his words. My heart clenches, and tears prick behind my eyes.

"Some days, a lot. And some days I don't even feel it."

He nods his head. "Tell me."

"I don't want to," I say and my throat's hoarse, making my

words crack. I don't. I've tried to talk about it before; I just can't.

"Well, there's what happened because of me. That's adding to it."

"Yes. It is." I can't lie. I'm not fucking okay. What they did to me was horrific, and I'm shocked I survived it. But I survived because I fought. And I'm damned proud of that.

"And your ex," he says softly, and guilt eats away at me. I should be grieving more for him. I turn away from him and settle my back against his chest. I'm not responding to that. I don't want to.

"Doll?" he asks before kissing my neck. "You really think you'll be alright?" I consider his words.

"Some days I'm overworked and high stressed, and I can't seem to figure anything out. But I only need to make it one day at a time. Some moments I remember, and it's too much. But most of the time I'm alright. I can be okay. I can live through this. I can continue to live through anything, I suppose."

He's quiet for a long time. So long I think maybe he fell asleep and I close my eyes, waiting for sleep to take me.

"I wish I could take it all away." His chest vibrates against my back as I register his words.

"You do more than you know." It's true. I feel... alive. I haven't felt so much in months. So much desire. I mostly just run through to-do lists. Other than that, there's just Jax. Jax has kept me sane. "Jax makes it all worth it, you know?" He makes me want to smile. And I read somewhere that if you smile enough, it will make you happy. You can't help it. It's biology or something. "If I didn't have Jax, I don't know that I would've survived it all."

"I hope you know how strong you are, Becca." *Strong?* I wouldn't call myself strong. Tears prick at my eyes again. I don't ever feel strong. I feel so weak. I feel like I'm holding on to nothing, grasping for a thread that's taunting me. Tears leak from the corners of my eyes, and I try to wipe them without him knowing. But he sees. He rises from behind me and kisses away the tears on my cheek and chin.

"I didn't mean to make you cry, doll." A heavy sob wracks through my body. I don't know why I'm crying. I don't want to cry. My throat closes as another sob leaves me, and I bury my face in my hands. "Let it out, doll. It's okay, I've got you." I turn in his arms and cry into his chest. His strong arms wrap around me and hold me close.

"You're alright, doll. I've got you." His hands run up and down my back in soothing strokes as he kisses my hair. His loving touch is so unexpected. Everything about him is unexpected.

His hot breath on my neck makes my entire body shiver. Another kiss, this time on the tender spot just below my ear. I feel wrapped in his presence. Secure in his embrace. Something in me cracks. My armor falls. I feel myself melt into him.

I feel a need to be comforted by him. A need I only caved to once years ago. It's haunted me and left a deep hurt in my chest that I've grown used to. It tightens and twists, threatening to consume me. A mix of loneliness and insecurity. It fucking hurts. And feeling his arms around me, soothing me, the familiar pain pangs in my chest. I need this. I need him.

I feel a spark ignite deep in my core, and a haze of lust comes down around me. It's the same sensation when we first met in his office. My lips part at the memory of when he took me against the wall. I turn and push my breasts against his hard chest. My hand cups the back of his head, and my lips press against his gently. He moans into my mouth as his tongue tastes mine. His fingers spear my hair before fisting it at the nape of my neck. He pulls back, and his light blue eyes look deep into mine.

My breath hitches, and my body's overcome with a feeling of ice pricking my heated nerve endings. A chill goes through me as he searches my face for something. *Please don't reject me.* I need this. I whimper as he pulls my hair back and leaves open-mouth kisses along my jaw and down my neck.

Relief washes through me, and the heat in my core rages with need. I rock my pussy against his thigh for relief. His firm hand pushes my hip down onto the mattress as he climbs on top of me. He never lets up the kisses on my neck. His hands roam my body, down my waist, my hips. He parts my legs and settles between them and pulls back to look down on me.

"You're so fucking beautiful." I close my eyes and drop my head against the pillow. I'm in dangerous territory. My heart is begging for more. I'm only going to end up hurt. I know it. But I want it. I want him. I need him.

I open my eyes and find him shirtless, his ripped abs and corded muscles enhanced by the shadows in the dark. His hands grip my hips before traveling up my belly, his thumbs pulling my shirt. I lift my back and let him pull the shirt over my head, baring myself to him. His mouth immediately comes down as he sucks a nipple into his mouth and palms my other breast. His hot tongue massages my hardened peak and my back arches, pushing more of myself into him.

His deft fingers twist my other nipple. The hot sensation is directly linked to my clit. A whimper escapes me. I brush my heat against his hard cock. Too much fabric between us. I need more. My heels dig into the mattress, needing more friction. His teeth bite down gently as he pulls away from me. His grasp on the other breast becomes nearly violent as he pulls back, giving a hint of pain that only adds to the intense pleasure. A wave of heat travels down my body.

His other hand steadies my hip, and then I hear a tear and feel the pull of the lace fabric against my skin.

I force my eyes open as his fingers slip through my slick folds. His broad shoulders and heated gaze portray him as a man of sheer dominance and lust. He stares deep into my eyes as his fingers dip into my heat and his thumb presses against my clit.

My body shudders beneath the pleasure of his touch. His

fingers pump in and out of me relentlessly, and his thumb pushes down harder. A tingle of heat travels through every limb in an instant and I convulse underneath him, held down only by the weight of his hand splayed on my hip. I hold in my scream, opening my mouth and throwing my head back. The sheer intensity of my orgasm nearly paralyzes my body. My body goes limp with pleasure, and I finally breathe.

Dom's lips take mine with passion as he lies on the bed, pulling my back to his chest. He sucks and nibbles my bottom lip while I try to breathe, my chest heaving for air and breaths coming in pants. He pushes into me, slowly and deep. His girth stretches my walls. One of his arms wraps around my shoulders and his hand massages my breast, while the other cradles my leg, parting my legs for him further. He pushes in and out of me deliberately slow, but deep. All the while kissing me. My moans are trapped in his kiss.

My head falls back as my pussy clamps around his dick and that hot wave travels through my body with a vengeance. A strangled cry leaves my lips. His hand grips my chin and tilts my lips to his. But they only touch as he stares into my eyes and pumps into me. Faster and harder, forcing the numbing tingles through my limbs, building with a crippling intensity at my core. His hand moves to my clit and he brushes his fingers on the sensitive nub without mercy, sending me over the edge. His gaze keeps mine as I cum violently, my body trembling in his arms while he continues to pump into me, rutting with a primal need until he finds his own release.

My chest warms, and my body opens to him as he gently settles my body and continues to kiss me with a passion I'm not sure I've ever known. I turn in his embrace as best I can, just wanting to be held.

I try to calm my breathing. My trembling hands rest against his corded arm wrapped around my waist. He gently kisses down my jaw, down my neck. His open-mouth kisses leave a warmth that quickly turns to chills as the air hits them.

My breathing finally slows, and I turn in his arms. He holds me close against his chest. My eyes open as I watch his chest rise and fall as he calms his own breathing. I hear his heart beating loudly, yet with a steady rhythm. It's hypnotizing.

A mix of relaxation and security warms my chest; my heart makes me weak. I swallow the lump growing in my throat and try to push down the emotions threatening to overwhelm me. I press my forehead to his chest as my back shudders from the cool air.

Dom reaches down and grabs his shirt from the floor for me. I give him a small smile and quickly put it on.

This is dangerous. Too emotional. I'm too weak to be playing these kinds of games. It's not like it was before, where I could just walk away. Where I could live a fantasy and then return to my reality. My heart beats louder and chaotically against my chest. It doesn't trust me, and I don't trust it.

His brow furrows, and his eyes narrow. Just as he asks,

"What's wrong?" I hear Jax in the other room.

"Mommy!" he calls out as though he's lost.

Dom slides easily off the bed and reaches for his pants. "Stay here; I'll get him," he says as though it'd be alright for him to go to my son. Jax pushes the door open as I open my mouth to stop Dom.

"Hey little man, Mommy's tired right now, can I read you a bedtime story?" he asks in a sweet voice I didn't know could be uttered from his lips.

My heart beats faster and tries to climb up my throat as he bends down so he's eye level with Jax. Jax's sleepy eyes focus on Dom as he runs a hand through his hair. He lets out a small yawn and nods his head.

The word escapes my lips and echoes off the walls, "Red!" The two look up at me, both with confusion. And then the realization dawns across Dom's face. My heart crumples in my chest. My throat dries, and a soreness leaks through every inch of my body.

I press my lips together and hold back the sobs threatening me, hating myself. Tears leak out of the corners of my eyes as I climb carefully off the bed, keeping the shirt down and walk silently to Jax. My hands shake as they go to his shoulders.

Guilt consumes me.

My heart may believe that what Dom and I just shared was something more than a quick, dirty fuck. But logically, I know better. I swallow thickly, avoiding Dom's gaze. I know it was one-sided. And it was stupid. I keep doing stupid things around this man.

But not when it comes to Jax.

"It's alright baby, I'll read you a story." I'm almost surprised how easily and calmly the words flow from my lips. But then I remember I've been doing this for quite some time now, hiding the pain and being strong for my son.

Only I don't remember it ever hurting this much.

CHAPTER 19

DOM

I can't fucking sleep. She ripped my fucking heart out. How the fuck am I supposed to react to that? I'm trying real fucking hard not to take offense to that. That's where she draws the line? I can fuck her all I want. Talk about using her pussy as payment, and fucking make love to her in my bed. But I can't read her kid a bedtime story?

She had no fucking underwear on. My cum was probably leaking down her thigh. But she'd rather that?

She fucking safe worded me. I've only been safe worded a handful of times when I first started playing. I know limits. I know what women want. I'm good at reading their body language. But I can't read her, my doll. Just thinking of my pet name for her has my heart clenching in agony.

I'm a fucking fool for thinking she's mine. She's not meant to be with a man like me, and it's obvious she wants it to stay that way.

I thought she felt it. How could she not? I gave her everything. I feel raw and broken. And now she's lying next to me right where I fucked her, on her side with her back to me, pretending to sleep. I know she's awake. Her breathing isn't even close to steady.

I'm not gonna do this. I'm not going to put up with this shit.

She wants to act like that, it's on her. But my heart is fucking open, and I'm not going to let her pretend I didn't just make love to her. That I didn't just see right into her fucking soul as she came on my dick. It was fucking beautiful. I'm not going to let her disrespect that.

"Why are you pretending to sleep, doll?" I ask, doing my best to keep the contempt out of my voice.

"I'm not pretending." Her voice comes out confident, and then lowers. "Just trying to sleep."

"You don't want me to hold you after tonight?" That fucking hurts, too. I should be all over her. Making sure she's alright. I know better than to let her be on her own. But fuck, I'm hurting after that shit.

"It's alright if you don't want to." Her voice breaks at the end. My brows raise in surprise.

"Babe?" I lean over and turn her so her back is on the bed. Her cheeks are tearstained. Fuck! "Doll, what's wrong?" I pull her into my embrace, and she fucking loses it. "Have you been crying this whole time?"

"No." She shakes her head into my chest and barely gets the word out.

"Let it out, babe." I gently rub her back and feel like a fucking prick. I've been lying here pissed because she doesn't want me around her son, yet she's been crying right next to me and I didn't even know. "Tell me what's wrong." I speak gently, but firmly. I know she's gonna try to find a way around telling me what's bothering her. My heart twists in agony; she didn't want me to know she was crying.

"I know this is going fast babe, but you gotta try to trust me."

A sob leaves her as she shakes her head. "It's alright babe, just let it all out."

"I can't." She pushes away from me with tears in her red-rimmed eyes. Her plush lips are turned down, and I still think she looks so damn beautiful. I don't know how I ever looked at her before as just a piece of ass. But something's different now.

"You can, babe. Just let it out."

She shakes her head and her chest heaves with a sob, her shoulders bowing inward. "I can't with you." She sucks in a strangled breath. "This," she says, motioning between us, "I can't." Her voice chokes on the last word. And it may as well have choked me.

My chest hollows and I let out a heavy breath, wrapping my arm around her shoulders and letting her cry into my chest. I don't think I've ever felt pain like this. I don't fucking like it.

"You don't wanna be with me, doll?" I need her to say the words. I don't want to hear them, but I need her to say them.

"That's not it." A spark of hope flares in my chest until she adds, "Jax." My breath stops short. "I can't do this to Jax," she cries into my chest.

"Because I'm in the mob?" I ask clearly somehow.

"I can't give him that life." She shakes her head, and I hardly hear her words through her tears.

I swallow the lump growing in my throat. "You don't think I'd be good for him?" I'd be great for him. I don't know much about kids, but I'd learn. I'd treat them both better than her shit husband did.

She pulls away from me and looks at me with disbelief. "How could you?" She wipes the tears away with the back of her hand and tries to get off the bed. I snatch her wrist and pull her closer to me. I take her lips with mine and push her back onto the mattress. One hand on her throat and one beside her head, bracing my body. I cage her in and kiss her with everything I have. Her fingernails dig into my back.

I bite down on her bottom lip and pull back until she whimpers. I whisper in the air between us, "I'm good enough to fuck, but that's it?"

A sad look of regret crosses her face. I wish it hadn't. I

don't want to be a regret. I know I gave her what she needed. "Is that it, doll?" I search her pained expression for anything other than regret and remorse. "You don't want me, babe?"

Her lips part, and the saddest noise sounds from her lips. I can see in her eyes that she wants me. I know she trusts me from the way her hand gentles on my forearm. My hand's wrapped around her throat, and she doesn't even react to it. I lean down and kiss her again, closing my eyes and gently sucking. I brush my tongue along the seam of her lips and she parts them, opening herself for me and moaning into my mouth.

She fucking loves me like I do her. It's not supposed to be like this, but what really ever happens like it's supposed to?

I gently rest my forehead against hers. My body heats, and my dick hardens with a desperate need to be inside her again and show her how much she loves me.

"Don't fucking act like you don't want me." My hips push her legs apart, and she opens them obediently. "You just don't want to believe you do." I rock my dick against her heat before reaching down to push my pants down. "Stop lying to yourself."

"I do." She struggles to say her words. Relief washes through me, but it's only temporary. The look on her face tells me everything. She'll never be with me. It fucking hurts. She didn't even give us a chance. She must see my pain, because her hands grab my neck and she pushes my lips onto hers.

"Please," she whispers. But I don't know what she means. I can't ever figure her out. I look deep into her hazel eyes.

"Please," she asks again, her breathing shallow. She bites her bottom lip and rocks against my hard dick.

She just wants me to fuck her. A sharp shot to my chest makes me almost get off her, but her words stop me.

"Like you want to. Like I'm yours." I barely hear her words. I search her eyes and then I hear the sweetest sounds whispered from her lips, "Punish me."

It won't take the pain away. I know it won't, but I'll be damned if I don't want to pin her down and make her love me.

I narrow my eyes and look down at Becca. "Take your shirt off and get on your knees."

I'm going to take her exactly how I've wanted to since I first held her ass in my office. It may be the last time I ever get to. In the morning I know she'll want to leave. And I don't think I have it in me to stop her. So I'm going to make this night count. I sit back on my heels and stroke my dick as she obeys me.

My hand comes down hard across her ass, leaving an angry red print. She yelps, and her body jolts forward with the blow. The slap echoes through the room, and then I remember her son. Fuck! I need to be quiet. A small voice inside me says she's right. But I push that shit down and shake it off. I reach into the nightstand for some lube with my right hand while my left rubs the mark on her ass. I can have her tonight. Every way I want, and every way she wants.

I lean forward, my dick nestled between her heat and take her throat in my hand. I squeeze lightly and whisper into her ear, "You want me to fuck you like you're mine to do what I want, how I want."

I stroke the lube over my dick and use the excess over her puckered hole. I don't waste any time slipping my finger in knuckle deep. "Good girl. Arch your back," I say and she immediately obeys. "Push back, babe." I fuck her ass with my finger until she's moaning into the pillows, and then I add a second. My left hand strokes my dick, and I wish it was in her mouth. Her lips are parted, and soft whimpers are falling easily from them. Her eyes are closed, and I know she's enjoying this. I pull my fingers out and line my dick up; her eyes fly open, and it makes me smirk.

"This is what you want from me, babe?" I keep my hand on the small of her back to keep her steady, and I watch those lips turn into a perfect "O" as I pump shallow thrusts into her ass. Her hot walls feel so fucking good. She clenches her heat as her head thrashes on the pillow.

"You want me to fuck you like I own you," I say and lean down and push my dick deep into her, all the way to the balls. "Guess what, doll?" I pull back, almost all the way out. My dick begs to be back in her warmth. Her ass looks so fucking perfect with my dick in it. I grab her chin in my hand and pull her head back so she has to look at me. "I do own you."

I slam back into her and watch her beautiful lips part with a cry of pleasure. I keep up a steady pace, holding her eyes. My breathing comes in pants as I fuck her exactly how she wants. She wants it brutal; she wants to believe that's who I am. I'll give her that. I won't deny her. I thrust into her, and I don't hold back. Her breasts bounce with my movements and I reach forward to cup one and squeeze it and pull to give her the added sensation. Her mouth hangs open, and her eyes squeeze shut as I keep up my pace. Her whimpers turn to squeaks, and I know she's getting close. My hand flies to her clit as a cold sweat breaks out on my body.

"Cum for me." Her back bows, and her head falls to the mattress as she does exactly what I told her to do. My balls draw up, and my spine tingles as I find my own release with hers. I pump into her with every wave until the aftershocks have passed.

I gently pet Becca's back and kiss her shoulder. "Stay here, doll." I plant another kiss on her shoulder and grab a hand towel from the bathroom to clean up. I wipe both of us off and lay her gently on the bed. I wasn't gentle with her. Not like I was planning to be at her place.

I lie down beside her and pull her into me. None of that crying on her own shit. Tonight she's mine. "You alright, babe?" I ask as she backs her ass up to nestle between my hips. It makes a soft smile form on my lips.

"Hmmm." She's so exhausted she can't even answer. I rub my hand down her arm and kiss her shoulder before settling behind her. Her warm body against mine feels so right.

A pang pains in my chest at the thought, and just as I

close my eyes and pray for sleep to take me, I hear her say it. "I love you, Dom." It's mumbled from her lips. I prop myself up on my elbow and look at her. She's peacefully asleep, but I know I heard her say it.

I lie back down and kiss her hair. "I love you, doll." I whisper the words and pray maybe that will be enough.

CHAPTER 20

DOM

I can't stop watching her fuss over her little boy. They're in my kitchen, sitting at the island eating breakfast. I lean back against the granite, gripping it to keep me in place. I could see myself with them. I could see myself with one arm wrapped around her waist, and my other hand messing up Jax's hair. An asymmetric grin pulls at my lips as she leans over to fix his hair. It makes me want to mess it up even more.

I can see the three of us together. But she can't. Or won't. I don't know which.

I push off the counter to walk over to her, but my phone goes off. It catches Becca's attention, and she looks at me with anxiety in her eyes. She's been asking to go home since she woke up. She's been avoiding me, and not letting me touch her.

Well, she doesn't move away from me, but she stills in my arms. She doesn't mold to me and thrive in my embrace like she did last night. I knew it would be like this. I just didn't know it would hurt this much.

"Yo." I answer the phone how I always do, but when her eyes fall to the counter and then to Jax, I wish I hadn't answered it at all.

"Got 'em," Johnny says, and I know exactly what he's talking about.

"How many?" He got De Luca and his crew. My fists clench, and my blood runs cold. I'm gonna beat the fucking piss out of them and make them suffer for what they did to my girl.

"All." An evil smirk forms on my face, and I have to walk out of the kitchen to hide it from her.

I remember what Becca said so I ask, "Is a dragon there?"

There's hesitation on the other end. I know I'm not supposed to ask detailed questions. It can always come back around if shit on the other end is heard.

"It's here. All of 'em." I nod my head and let out a sigh of relief. Her house is fine, untouched. I got that message when I woke up. And now De Luca is done. That's everything. Everything that's given me a reason to keep her to myself.

"Later."

"Later, boss," he answers quickly, and hangs up. Short

calls, that's the way they have to be.

My brow furrows as I pocket my phone and walk back into the kitchen. I grip the back of the chair that Becca's sitting in at the island. As soon as these fuckers are gone, there's no reason for me to keep her here.

My eyes travel to her son who gives me a happy smile before picking his bowl up and slurping the milk out. I know why she doesn't want me and it hurts, but she's right. I can't put her son through this life. I couldn't guarantee her safety, and I can't ask her to risk her son. A frown pulls at my lips, and I can't help it. It hurts. I don't want to say goodbye.

"Who was that?" I smirk at her. She's gotta learn to not ask so many questions. The smirk fades as I realize she doesn't. She doesn't have to learn shit; she's leaving me.

"That was what I needed to hear this morning." That's all I can really say to her. She's already seen too much. I won't risk her knowing any more.

"We can go home?" Her eyes widen with hope. It fucking shreds me.

"Yeah, doll. As soon as Jax is done with breakfast, I'll let you two go."

CHAPTER 21

BECCA

Everything hurts. Every last bit of me aches. But I won't take the pills. I want to feel the pain. My chest hurts the worst. The knot where my heart used to be just won't go away.

"Mommy!" Jax yells through the hall.

"Jax!" He's butt naked, and his towel is on his shoulders like a cape. I shake my head and try to hide my smile. This kid. "Baby, I told you to get your PJs on."

"I want sleepover." He's giving me those puppy dog eyes he always gives me. But that's something I can't cave on. That'll never happen again. I'm grateful he isn't anything but happy about everything. He has no idea. Thank fuck he's only three.

I squat down and hold back the wince from the slight pain in my ass. "We'll do another play date with Ava soon, okay?" I gently push the hair out of his face and wrap his towel around him.

He purses his lips and narrows his eyes at me, and I can't help but crack up laughing. "Bedtime, mister." I use my mommy voice, and he doesn't like that.

"Daddy never made me go bed." He pouts, and I have to hold everything back and try to think about what I read online. I'm coming up short. How to handle divorce. How to handle death. I don't remember. I can't think. I don't know what's best. My body heats with anxiety, and I have no idea how to respond to him.

"Fine!" He stomps his foot and crosses his arms. As soon as his back is turned, I stand and wipe the bastard tears from my eyes.

Fucking hell, could today get any worse?

Work was a disaster; I wish I'd just stayed away. Who the fuck am I kidding? Work was just like every other day. That's not what hurt about today.

I force myself to straighten my back and pick out a book to read for his bedtime story. "This one, baby?" I ask.

"I'm not a baby, Mom." He huffs and lies back on the bed. "I'm three." He holds up three fingers and speaks with exasperation. I wish I wasn't so fucking emotional, because that really hurt. I want to scream. I want to cry. But instead

I ask, "Okay *Jax*, this one?"

He smiles and nods his head, and it takes everything in me to sit on his bed and pretend like I'm not falling to pieces. I read him the fairytale with the same peppy voice, although my throat feels hoarse and raw. The only thing keeping me together is hearing his little voice tell me he loves me as he hugs me before I get off the bed. He may not think he's my baby boy, but he is. I hold him longer than I have in a long time, and he lets me. My heart clenches, and I have to give him a kiss and turn out the lights quickly before he sees what a mess I am.

As soon as I shut the door, I let it all out.

I cry harder than I have for years and I stumble into my room, exhausted and wishing I could change everything.

Three loud knocks at the door stir me from my sleep. Shit. I'm still fully clothed and lying on my stomach over the made bed. I wipe under my eyes and slowly climb off the bed, feeling exceptionally unsteady.

Bang! Bang! The knocks pound on the door. I practically jog to the door so the banging doesn't wake up Jax. Who the fuck is banging at this hour? Anger gets the best of me, and I almost swing the door open without looking. It isn't even locked. I grind my teeth and nearly snap when whoever it is bangs on the other side again. I need to get a grip and be smart. I stand on my tiptoes to see clearly out of the peephole.

It's a cop. Fuck!

My heart sputters, and my fingertips go numb. I shake them out and open the door before that fucker decides to knock again.

"Rebecca?" he asks with concern apparent in his voice.

"Yes, that's me." I want to correct him, but I don't; technically that's my name. I just fucking hate not being called Becca.

"I'd like to speak with you if you have a moment." His eyes search my face and then behind me. I almost look over my shoulder, but stop myself. I know there's no one there.

I nod my head and say, "Sure." But I don't move an inch. We can have this conversation right here, and real fucking quick.

"We had a call this evening that you and your son were kidnapped and held against your will," he says far more calmly than I would imagine possible.

I huff a humorless laugh. "Well obviously that's not true. I'm standing right here." My fingers itch to touch my chin. To make sure the makeup is still covering the bruises.

The officer shifts uncomfortably in front of me. "Where were you yesterday?" My mouth stays shut as I look him in the eyes.

"I was with a friend."

"Could I have that friend's name?" He takes out a pad and a pen from his back pocket and I want to smack it away.

"Am I being charged with anything?" I make sure that

my voice echoes annoyance. I'm not annoyed. I'm scared shitless. I don't want him here asking questions.

"Not unless you're lying. Are you withholding any information?" The officer's strong jaw juts out, and he looks past my shoulder again.

"No, I'm not. I'd like to go to bed, officer." My grip on the door tightens as I add, "I'm fine. There's no reason to waste either of our time. I'm exhausted and just want to go to bed." That last part is the truth at least.

"May I come in to take-" I don't let him finish.

"I'd rather you didn't. My son's asleep." There's no fucking way I want him in here.

"I completely understand, Mrs. Harrison." Hearing that name makes anger course through me.

"Bartley now."

"I'm sorry?" he asks.

"Rebecca Bartley. Harrison was my married name."

"Oh. My apologies. Have a good night now." He seems sincere, but that doesn't damper my anger. Or my sadness.

I give him a tight smile. "You, too." I'm surprised the overwhelming emotion I'm feeling is anger. It's followed closely by a deep aching hurt in my gut.

I close the door, turning both locks and lean my back against it. My eyes fall shut, and I try to breathe.

I can't do this shit on my own.

I wish Dom were here. I wish he could hold me. I wrap

my arms around my shoulders and walk slowly to bed, feeling lost and unsure and very much alone.

CHAPTER 22

DOM

I clench and unclench my hands to get rid of the numbness. It makes the cuts open, and it fucking hurts like hell. But I don't give a shit. I'm glad it hurts.

"You alright, boss?" Johnny keeps fucking asking me the same damn question every hour. No. I'm not alright.

"I'm fine." When I register what I've answered, I snort a laugh. That's what she'd say.

I take a seat at the desk in the corner of the office. It's on the opposite side of the room, across from the pool table. It's a sleek-looking glass desk with steel trimmings. I don't think I've ever sat here. My fingers tap along the glass top, waiting for our next drop.

It's so fucking tedious. So damn boring. I don't need to do this shit. I've got more money than I'd ever wanted, and nothing to spend it on. What the fuck did I even use to do sitting here?

"Boss?" I look up with a scowl, and then feel like a prick. It's not his fault. But then again, I am a prick.

I take in a deep breath and manage to sound somewhat normal. "What?"

"Just wanted you to know you still have those requests."

"What requests?" I ask.

"To sell out if you wanted to." My forehead pinches in confusion. What the fuck is he talking about? He answers before I have to ask. "I know you said to stop bringing it up, but I just thought you might like to know."

That's when it clicks. Give my business over to those thugs? I'm always getting shit offers. They don't want to pay the right amount to take my clients, and they'd ruin this shit anyway. They don't know what they're doing like I do. "Pass." That's an easy decision.

Johnny gives me a tight smile and nods. "Just thought maybe you'd rather do something else now." He takes a seat on the sofa, staring at the field. A few players are out running gauntlets; fucking sucks to be them.

Do something else. Like what? Just run the books for my Pops? That'd be boring as hell. I never really wanted to do anything other than make a name for myself. Get laid, and get paid. That was my motto for the longest time. But now I don't fucking want it anymore. I don't want this. Maybe I will sell the business. Maybe she'd want me then.

I shake my head and rap my knuckles across the glass tabletop; no she won't. It doesn't change a damn thing about who I am. I know it, and she knows it.

But I'm the boss' son. He tried to keep me out of the life, but I demanded my way in. You can't leave the family. Sure as fuck not when you're the boss' son. My chest hurts just thinking that. I'll never be the kind of man Becca deserves. I was born into the mob. There's only one way out, and I'm not ready to die.

A knock at the door distracts me from my morbid thoughts. I sigh and click my phone on. Ten a.m. Too fucking early. This day needs to get going so I can get home. I'll figure out a reason to be there when the time comes. I just don't want to be here.

Johnny opens the door, and my pops' voice booms through the hall.

"Johnny!" I raise my eyes to watch, although I don't lift my head. Pops pats him on the back and gives him a warm smile. But it's off. He's waiting to hear about Clara. I know he is. Something's going on between the two of them. Not my business though. Not unless he hurts her. Then I'll make it my business.

"Good to see you, boss." Johnny makes eye contact and returns the smile. Ballsy. Johnny is most certainly ballsy. He's been a friend of mine for years, and I sure as shit couldn't do this business without him. But I don't like that he's sneaking around with my sister. And I sure as shit know that Pops doesn't like it. He better give it up soon and put a ring on her finger.

"Hey Pops." I lean back in my seat and then stand to greet him. "Didn't know you were coming."

We share a quick hug and I motion to the liquor, but he shakes his head.

He takes a casual seat on the sofa, and I relax in the spot next to him. He's come here a few times, usually because we're meeting up for a family event... or a *family event.* But I always know about it ahead of time.

"What's going on, Pops?"

"I just wanted to make sure you're doing alright." He looks me in the eyes, and I almost look away. I lean forward and rest my elbows on my knees and set my chin on my clasped hands. I take a moment to answer him. I don't know what to tell him. I'm not okay.

I settle on what I hope is the truth. "I'll be alright."

"That was intense, Dom. Never seen you like that." I gaze at the floor and take a deep breath in, followed by a long exhale.

"Yeah, well." What's he want me to say? My memory flashes back to a few nights ago, to my fists beating the piss out of them. They were tied down when I got there. Just like they tied her down. I saved the one with the dragon tattoo for last. I wanted to make sure he knew what was coming.

I wanted him to watch the rest of them die. De Luca was second to last. No one gave a fuck that I took the lead.

I needed to. I had to. For her.

"Sean went to see her the other night. Rebecca." Hearing her name brings me back to the present.

"It's Becca. And I know." His brows raise in surprise, and his lips turn down.

"She called you?" he asks.

"No, I went over there. Just to tell her she was safe." My gut churns, and my heart freezes in my chest. I wanted to go up there and talk to her, to convince her to just give it a chance. But I'd be a fucking asshole to do that to her and Jax. They deserve better. So I stayed in my car. Thinking about what a prick I am for wanting her. "I saw him walk up, and I waited."

"Well, what'd she tell you about it?" Pops leans into me.

I shake my head. "Nothing." I swallow the lump in my throat and lick my lips before sitting back in my seat. "I didn't talk to her."

"Ah." Pops looks to the left at Johnny and then sighs. "Well," he turns back to me, "she didn't give away anything. So she's cleared. I told Jack to back off."

"What the fuck is Jack saying now?" My blood heats, and anger stirs inside of me hearing that shit. Back off? He better fucking back off.

"Nothing, Dom." Pops puts his hand on my shoulder. "He's just paranoid as fuck. He's happy now."

I search his eyes and nod. "He better be fucking happy. She may never be mine to claim, but she's off limits."

"I don't understand, Dom." He lowers his voice and looks at me with a sad expression. "Is it 'cause she's got a kid? He's a good little guy, and he's-"

I rear my head back to look at him. "That's not it. That's not it at all."

"I don't get it, Dom. What the hell's a matter with you?" It's been a while since my father has talked to me that way.

I chew on the inside of my lip not wanting to say it, but he asked. And he's the boss. "She's got to protect her son. She can't be messing around with me."

"I didn't say anything about messing around, Dom. I saw the way you two looked at each other. What you did for her. I know what she means to you. And you're just going to let her go?"

"I have to. She can't live this kind of life." I wave my hand in the air and sit back with a heavy weight on my chest. My hand runs down my face.

"Then give it up. If you think she's worth it."

"Give up the *familia*?" I can't believe what he's saying.

He purses his lips and sucks in a deep breath. "That's not what I meant. Get outta this here. Lay low. Get a boring ass day job with your degree. Do what you gotta do."

"Do what I gotta do?" I swallow hard. I don't like subtleties. I'd rather be smacked hard in the face with a blunt answer.

"I can't tell you any more than that, son. I will say Sunday dinner will always be at our house with the family."

"What's that have to do with anything?"

"Just make sure she knows that's a condition. The only condition." *The only condition.* I stare at my Pops for a moment.

He gives me a smile and rises, fixing his suit jacket. "Your ma liked her. That's a huge victory there."

"I don't think it's as easy as you think, Pops." I stand up and give him a quick hug with a firm grip.

"If you want her to be yours, then you take her; what's so hard about that?" He smirks at me and then turns his back and leaves.

I watch the door close shut. If only it could really be that easy.

Chapter 23

Becca

The dishes in the large steel sink crash together, and it draws my eyes up to the busboy. He's new. His arms are skinny as twigs. His eyes dart to mine and then back to the dishes.

"Break any?" I ask lightheartedly to put him at ease. I try to muster up a smile, but I can't.

"Don't think so." He pulls them out carefully, one by one.

At least it wasn't at the bar. That would've been a pain in the ass. Like yesterday. I close my eyes and breathe in deep. I wish I still had Vicky here. She was one of the managers Dom put in charge while I was "recovering from a fall." I roll my eyes and rub my shoulder as I walk out of the kitchen to the back room. I had to dump her though. I didn't trust her or the others. I felt like they were always watching me. Like they were going to report back to him.

Just thinking about him has my chest tightening with pain. I haven't heard a word. Nothing. Tears prick my eyes. I know I didn't want it, well I didn't want to want it. But fuck, I do want *him*. I shake my head and try to calm myself down. My throat seems to close up every time I think about him. It physically hurts me. I can't explain it. It wasn't supposed to be this way. I lean against the wall of my office and lay my head against the wall. I can't fucking breathe in here.

After a moment I push open the door to go outside. It groans, and the bright light makes my eyes squint. But at least it's fresh air. Or as fresh as it can be for a tiny ass alley between my restaurant and the gallery next door. I prop the door open with a brick and take a seat on the crates a few feet down, closer to the empty street and away from the dumpsters.

I wish I was over this by now. Over him. Everything seems so much harder since I left him. Exhaustion weighs down on me. But it's not just physical; I'm emotionally overwhelmed.

"You alright, doll?" My body jumps at the sound of a deep, masculine voice in the silent alley. A small scream of shock forces its way out of my mouth and my hands fly up to hold it in. *Dom.* He walks toward me down the alley with a sexy ass smirk on his face.

My heart swells in my chest, and the tears flow. I can't hold them back. Fuck my hormones. Fuck my emotions. I don't care.

He takes another step toward me, and I fall into his embrace. My body feels weak; my wretched heart hurts. "Don't cry, doll." His strong arms hold me tight, and I want to pretend I can have this forever. Just the thought combined with his masculine smell and his soothing strokes on my back has my heart beating calmly and my body relaxing. It feels so right, so natural.

This is what I've needed.

"What's wrong?" He pulls back slightly to look down at me. I don't even lift my head; I keep my chin firmly against his chest and just breathe. My fingers dig into his back, holding him to me, but also fearing he's going to leave. I've never felt so weak and vulnerable. I don't know why I can't stop, but I just don't want to let go.

I shake my head against his chest and press my lips together. After a long moment, I answer, "You shouldn't be here."

"I want you, Becca." I finally pull away and stare into his eyes. I want him too, but I can't.

"You know I can't." I whisper the words. I know he understands. He has to understand.

"But you want to. I can make it right, doll. I'm just asking for a chance."

I want to. He's right about that. My breathing grows shallow. I open my mouth, but nothing comes out. A chance. Just one chance. Could I risk that?

"Let's make a bet," he says with a grin.

I snort and reply, "I'm not stupid; you're a bookie."

"It can be anything you want, babe." His smile softens, and he kisses my lips tenderly. "Just bet me." His lips barely touch mine.

"What do you get if you win?" I ask him with clear hesitation in my voice.

His hand travels to my ass and squeezes as he says, "You know what I want." I repress my moan and try to ignore how my core heats at his playful touch. I shake my head and bite down on my bottom lip to restrain my smile.

"Well, what do I get if I win?" I finally ask, looking up at him through my thick lashes.

My voice is breathy, and I wish it wasn't. I wish I wasn't so desperate for his comfort, but I am.

Dom's hand cups my chin, and his thumb runs along my bottom lip. His body brushes against mine as he takes a step forward, backing me into the brick wall. "Exactly what you want." My hands go to his chest, and I push him back slightly.

"Not here," I whisper into his mouth as his hands push my blouse up my waist. The cool air feels so wrong against my heated skin.

"You don't want me to fuck you against this wall, doll?" My pussy clenches with need, and moisture gathers in my core. Fuck yes I want it. "I need you, babe; it's been too long since I've had my dirty girl."

"I can't." I tilt my neck farther as he kisses down my throat to my shoulder. This is so bad, so wrong. But I want it. His breath, his kisses, his touch – they're everything I want. I want him to take me however he wants, whenever he wants. I want my back to scrape against the hard brick as he pounds into me. I can picture it so clearly. His hips keep me pinned with his hard-as-steel erection digging into my belly.

And then he stops. I nearly fall over from the loss of his touch. My body tilts forward, and I stumble in my heels and barely catch my footing. I hear Dom's hard steps on the pavement, his body slamming into something. Another man. I hear them barrel into the wall and fall hard on the ground. Fuck! Someone saw us! Shit, shit, shit.

I adjust my shirt and try to see what's going on. What the fuck is going on? I try to catch my breath.

"Dom, stop!" I yell out as I watch him push the man down on his stomach and twist his arm behind his back. I don't know him. No one fucking comes out here. My body heats with anxiety.

Dom grips his arm and shoves it up in an unnatural way. The man's face distorts with pain. Holy fuck! Fuck, he's really hurting him. "Stop!" I screech with a hoarse voice. My hands cover my mouth when I spot the gun falling from the stranger's grasp. Then I see what he's wearing; leather gloves, all black. *A gun complete with a silencer.* My heart drops to my gut. He was going to shoot Dom. My body goes cold and numb.

My feet naturally take a step back, and my body bumps into the brick wall. I can't turn away. I can't stop watching. I feel paralyzed as Dom relentlessly smashes the man's face into the concrete. The crushing sound of his bones crashing against the unforgiving ground makes me sick to my stomach. Oh my God. My breathing comes in short, shallow pants. I can't. I can't watch this.

"Not you! Wasn't you!" The man tries to speak. His face is distorted, covered in dark red with more blood bubbling from his busted lips.

"Who? Tell me who." Dom speaks hard and low into the man's ears, but I hear it as though he screamed it.

"The girl." *The girl.* Me.

"Who hired you?" Dom asks. My head goes dizzy watching the scene play out.

"Jack." The man's head sways, and then he takes in a hiss of breath as Dom pulls his arm back even further. And then Dom lifts the gun to the back of his head and pulls the trigger. The man falls forward, the raw bullet hole open and spilling blood onto the pavement.

My vision flashes before my eyes over and over again. No sound. No warning. He was alive, and now he's dead.

My eyes widen as I watch Dom shove the man behind the dumpster. There's blood everywhere. Holy fuck. Holy fuck. Holy fuck. Time passes in slow motion. It doesn't feel real. This can't be real.

The bang of the thin metal walls of the dumpster brings me back from the haze.

He's dead. I stare at the limp body. He was going to kill me. But Dom killed him first.

My throat closes, and I struggle to breathe. "What are we going to do?" my voice croaks. He's dead. Dom just shot him. "It was in self-defense." My voice raises, "You were only defending me!"

"Hush, doll." Dom walks to me with ease, gripping both of my arms at my side. "You don't have to worry about anything. The next people who come down this alley will be my clean-up crew. I already sent them a message."

What the fuck? I'm shaken and on edge. My body shivers as though I'm freezing. This is why we can't be together. *But if he hadn't been here...* My shaking hands cover my mouth. I would've died. I cry into my hands and barely realize Dom's dragging me away.

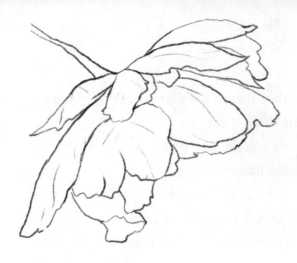

CHAPTER 24

DOM

That motherfucker! He's dead. And if they knew, if any of them knew – they're all fucking dead. I should've known better. My heart's still beating frantically in my chest. My blood's pumping with rage, but more than that, fear.

What if I hadn't been there? I was going to wait till she was done with work, till she'd put Jax to bed. I didn't want to risk her getting so damn worked up over me until she was alone. But then I saw her. I just had to go to her.

She was going through the motions; that's all. Her beautiful plump lips never turned up into her gorgeous smile. Every time her head fell in the slightest I swore she was crying.

How could I not go to her, knowing how hurt she was?

And it's a good fucking thing I did.

My hands grip the steering wheel, making my knuckles turn white. He was going to kill her. He didn't even fucking know her. A kill for pay. I saw him over her shoulder. Waiting. I fucking know who that bastard was, JD. He never asked questions, just got the job done. He wasn't family; he was an outside hire.

Well now he's fucking dead.

My body tingles and then heats. I need to beat the piss out of something. Like I did De Luca and his crew. I need to do that to Jack. He's probably at the bistro with my father.

Sitting together. Maybe my father knew. My heart crumples in agony, and I shake my head slightly in denial. My eyes peek at Becca, but thankfully she didn't notice. I don't want her to know how fucked up I am over this. That's not the way it's supposed to work.

My poor doll is staring out of the window wide-eyed. She hasn't fucking moved. Hasn't said a word. I wish she hadn't heard that, that she was the one he was supposed to kill. I wish she didn't know. It fucking kills me.

I grab my phone and dial my father. I can't wait to ask him in person. I need to know. I have to know right fucking now. The thought that he'd do that kills me. I just saw him yesterday. I don't understand why he'd do this to me. I shake my head again harder as the phone rings, and this time she sees. Her eyes are wide with worry.

"It's gonna be alright, babe." I breathe in deep and give her a forced smile. Her eyes fall, and she leans her head against the headrest, seemingly staring at nothing. Her lack of a response worries me.

"Dom. What's going on?" Pops answers like it's a normal call.

"You alone?" I want to make sure there's no one around to hear. Just in case. I don't want Jack to know I'm coming.

Pops talks over the phone to someone and the line is muffled for a moment, and then he comes back on and says, "All clear, Dom. What's going on?"

I swallow the lump in my throat and push the words through, "Did you know?" That's really what it comes down to. It's what I need to know.

I hear Pops move around on the other line, and then he speaks lower. "Dom, what's wrong? Where are you?" I stay silent for a moment and take in another deep breath. "You alright, Dom? You need something?"

"Did you know about the time on her?" Time is code for hit. The code varies, but right now that's what it means. His questions and his tone make me believe he didn't, but I want to hear him say it. I look at Becca with sad eyes; she's confused for a moment, and then tears fall down her cheeks and she quickly wipes them away. I know she understands.

"On your girl?" The sadness in his voice is mixed with disbelief. Then his anger comes through. "We'll find them, Dom."

"I know who." The callous words leave my lips without permission. I grind my teeth, waiting for him to ask.

"Who? We'll collect now." There's a moment of silence. "Is-" He pauses, and it's quiet for a second. "Is she alright, Dom?"

"Yeah. I was there."

"She's good?" The hope in his voice relaxes every doubt I had.

"Yeah, I got her."

"Thank fuck. Dom, you are one lucky son of a bitch. You know that?" I can hear the relief in his voice, but still there's pain.

"You all at the bistro now?" I ask.

"We're here, Dom. We'll get 'em."

"It was Jack." My father's silent. It fucking kills me to say it. We grew up with him. He was always there. The last few years, not so much. But growing up, he was like a second father to me and Vince. Tears prick at my eyes. I feel so fucking betrayed.

"Are you sure?" Pops' voice is deadly and low.

"That's what the fucker said. It was him." I straighten in my seat and brush it off as best I can. It's not the first time someone in the family has done some stupid shit. But it's the first time it's been directed at me.

"Jack's here. I'll question him and take care of it." I shake my head. That's not good enough.

"I wanna see him. I wanna look him in the eyes and know why."

"You know why, Dom; she knows a lot of shit." Before

I can respond, he adds, "Doesn't make it right in the least. He had his orders. He'll pay the price. I can't guarantee I'm gonna wait for you, Dom."

"I gotta get her home first." I can't bring her there.

"I know. You go take care of her."

"I wanna be there," I say one more time. I feel like he's not going to listen. Like he's gonna take him out himself.

"I understand. But I can't give you that right now, Dom. Just get her home and safe, and then call me. If I can, I'll come over."

I nod and say, "Alright," and hang up and try to relax somewhat. But I can't. I can't relax. A kill is a kill. It fucking sucks, and I've seen it over and over again. This one is different. This one's personal. That fucker was going to kill my girl. And Jack arranged it.

A long moment passes with silence. Jack's a dead man, and my Becca's safe. That's what matters.

"Babe, we're going to get through this." I reach across the console and grab her hand. I rub soothing circles on her soft skin. She keeps alternating between looking at me and out the window. I can tell she's scared, but other than that I have no idea what's going on in her head.

"The piece of shit that called the hit had no right." I try to keep her gaze, but she doesn't hold it. "Babe, you're safe. No one's ever going to hurt you again."

"You said that before." She barely speaks her words, and it shreds me. 'Cause it's true.

I wanted to go there and win her heart back with the promise of safety. And look what fucking happened. "It's over. I promise, everything will be fine, doll." Raising her small hand to my lips, I plant a small kiss on her tender wrist.

Her beautiful hazel eyes find mine, but all I can see in them is disbelief.

CHAPTER 25

BECCA

"Where is he?" Dom's furious. His corded muscles flex, and his voice echoes in the foyer. "You brought him here?" he asks incredulously as he slams the door. My body jumps from the loud bang. I don't even know how I got here. I feel like I just woke up from a dark clouded haze.

"Calm down, I wouldn't bring him to your home." His father's voice is calm, but it doesn't match his appearance.

I'm frozen at the door. I've only known this man for a week, and already two people have tried to kill me. One to get back at him, and one to protect him. My limbs feel limp and weak. The reality weighs heavy on me.

I wanted him. I was willing to try, to give it a chance like he asked.

"I just wanted to tell your Becca that she has nothing to worry about, regardless of whatever happens between you two." Although Dante's talking to Dom, his eyes are on me. He's obviously concerned and I suppose that's nice of him, but it just makes me feel uncomfortable.

I take in a staggered inhale and try to walk to them in the center of the foyer, but I can't. My feet are planted firmly in place. I'm stuck. Everything's so fucked.

His father takes heavy steps toward me, eating up the space between us. He's dressed in a suit with no tie. He looks distinguished, like a CEO. Nothing like the mob boss he is. "Everything's alright now. I promise you, no harm will come your way."

"Is he dead?" The question falls out of my mouth. I want to know. I *need* to know. I feel like there's a target on my back.

His eyes dart to Dom, and Dom gives a quick nod. "He will be."

"I'm gonna make him pay, doll." Dom's voice is hard and determined.

Make him pay. The images flash before me. The bullet hole, his bloodied face. I look away and cross my arms.

I change my mind.

I don't want to hear. I get it now. I understand why they keep their women out of it. I want out of it. I can't handle this shit. My mind keeps replaying the vision of the man's head smashing against the ground and falling limp with a bullet hole in the back of his skull. My body heats, and I feel faint. I swallow thickly and put my hand on my forehead.

I'm not okay. Ice pricks my skin, and my vision goes fuzzy.

"She's going into shock."

I shake my head. "I'm fine." Dom mumbles something under his breath, but I don't hear it.

He lifts me in his arms and carries me away. I don't even try to protest. "Just relax, babe; I got you."

I feel so fucking groggy. I rub my eyes and sit up in Dom's bed. Fuck, my head is killing me. I rub my temples as the pain radiates.

I rub my eyes and take a look around, and then I remember. My fists grip the sheets, and I sit up straighter with wide eyes. *Dom.* I need Dom.

"Relax, doll. I'm here." Dom walks into the room with a glass of water in one hand. "How are you feeling?"

"I don't know." I feel like shit. Everything feels like shit. I take the glass of water and take a sip, and then another. I greedily drain it, feeling a million times better.

He sits on the edge of the bed with his body turned toward me as I tap my nail against the glass.

"I can't do this, Dom. I can't run and hide. I can't put Jax through this shit." It physically hurts to say the words, but it's true. I need to end this.

"Tough, you need me now." His hard gaze dares me to disagree.

"That's not fair." My voice breaks.

"Life's not fair, babe."

"You got me into this shit, and now I can't leave." I shake my head and cover my face with my hands.

"That shit is over and done with." He grips my wrists and wraps my arms around his neck and pulls me into his lap. "That's not why you need me. You fucking love me, doll. You need me to love you, too."

I can't deny it; I love him. "But I can't."

"I'm not letting you go." Hearing his conviction eases my pain. He's making this decision. "No one's gonna fuck you the way I do."

A sad smile plays at my lips, and I huff a laugh as I wipe my eyes with the sleeve of my shirt.

"Can we leave? Please?" If he could take us away, I'd leave right now.

"You can't stop being family, doll." Fresh tears prick at my eyes, and my face heats. I should know better.

"I can't have Jax around this." I can't. I won't. That's not going to change.

"He won't be." Dom's answer is quick. "I'm selling the

business and getting a real job. I'm backing away from all of this shit." His fingers grip my chin, and he forces me to look him in the eyes as he says, "You want me to stop working for my dad, then I'll do it. If anyone can leave the *familia*, I can."

I shake my head. I know that's not how it works. "I have to go." I need to leave him. Before he leaves his family, before he risks his life.

"I'm not letting you leave. I told you; you're mine." I love how determined his words are. But it's not enough.

"I can't." My heart clenches and hollows with pain.

"You can. And you will. We'll do this together. And after today, I can't let you go. I refuse to let you leave me, doll."

My head shakes uncontrollably. "I just can't have Jax raised like this." My chest heaves for air as heat washes through my body. "I don't want this for him." Hot tears leak down my face.

"I know, doll." His thumb brushes a stray tear away as he looks at me with a sad smile.

"You know when I knew my family was a mob family?" he asks. "I found out when I was ten." A humorless laugh leaves him. "The journalists from the papers waited for me outside of school." A sad smile pulls at his lips. "I thought my pops ran a restaurant, that he was an entrepreneur."

His smile vanishes, and his hand leaves me. "The reporters told me he was a crook, a murderer." He says the words with distaste, practically spitting them. His eyes fall, and he swallows thickly. "I had no idea until then." He shifts and looks uncomfortably at the door as he adds, "Ma cried her eyes out. She couldn't even talk to me. Pops had to take me aside and tell me he had a business and when I wanted to know about it, he'd tell me." He forces a tight smile. "I never asked." He shakes his head. "Kids were always a little afraid of me at school, but other than that I think most things were normal. As far as I know."

He takes a deep breath and says, "The only time I thought my father was disappointed in me was when I told him I wanted to go to college for statistics. He never said it, but there was a look on his face. I asked him about it later, and he said he was so ashamed of himself in that moment. That he'd planned something else for me, and that it never occurred to him I deserved better."

"Got into Stanford, got my degree and a respectable job, and I fucking hated it. I can't lie, doll, I don't fucking like working." His tone makes a small laugh leave my lips. "So I came home, and Pops told me no. He told me I was more than a gangster. He told me I'd be better than him." A wicked grin grows across his face. "He was pissed when I told him I was a bookie. Didn't tell him for nearly a year. But I was having some problems and needed his help. That's when he let me in and gave me the books."

"What I'm saying is," he takes my hand in his and kisses the back of it, "I'm not the boss, doll. Our kids aren't gonna know until we tell them. And they don't have to be a part of this." His eyes plead with me to believe him. "They don't. I promise you." He kisses the back of my hand again and his sad eyes return to mine as he adds, "But if you want to leave, we'll go. Ma and the rest of the family will understand. You've already been through too much." He shakes his head with his eyes on the floor. We don't let our-" I crush my lips against his, and they're hard at first, caught by surprise, but he molds them to mine and then parts my lips with his tongue. I push my chest against his, needing to feel him. Needing his love more than my next breath.

I break our kiss and gasp for air. "I love you, Dom." Tears fall from the corners of my eyes. "I'm scared, but I fucking love you." I shake my head as he gently grabs my face with his hands.

His forehead rests against mine as his lips come down to meet me. "Tell me you'll stay with me. I promise I'll love you till the day I die."

"Yes, Dom. I love you. I just want to love you." His arms wrap around my body, pressing my breasts against his hard chest.

"I love you, doll. I love you and your son, so fucking much." My heart swells and pounds against my chest.

I know he does.

Epilogue

Becca

3 YEARS LATER

My house smells like heaven. I dip the wooden spoon into the sauce and blow lightly. I don't want to burn my tongue again like I did last time. I'm so damn impatient. I hesitantly taste it. Something's off. My lips purse, and my tongue clucks against the roof of my mouth.

"Your mother is a liar." I narrow my eyes at Dom, who smirks at me. "This is definitely not right." He walks over to me, looking hot as hell. Bare feet, jeans and no tee shirt. His muscles ripple as he strides toward me. I don't even bother trying to hide the fact that my eyes are glued to his body. Why should I give a fuck? If I wanna stare down my husband,

I'm going to do exactly that.

His large hand wraps around mine, and he takes a lick of the sauce seductively. Watching his tongue take a languid lick makes my pussy clench. I bite my bottom lip to keep in the moan as his hand travels to my hip. He gives me a cocky grin. That bastard. He knows what he's doing. We had a quickie this morning... and this afternoon.

"It's perfect, doll, your taste buds are just all fucked up with your hormones." He rubs my swollen belly and leans in to kiss me. I part my lips and moan into his mouth, greedily accepting his kiss. He pulls back and I'm slow to open my eyes, I'm just so tired. Not tired for sex though. My libido is ridiculous.

"Gross!" I smile and look over to the doorway of the kitchen, seeing Jax sticking his tongue out.

"Oh, yeah? I'll remind you that kissing is gross when you get older. Only six years old, guess kissing is pretty gross to you, huh?" Dom walks back to the island, leaving me with a view of his perfect ass. He puts his hand out and Jax gives him his homework, just like he does every day.

"That's my boy. Math is on point." Dom shuffles through the sheets before turning to look at Jax. "Where's English?"

"We had a substitute today," Jax answers with his chin resting on the counter. "Did it all during free period." I smile and turn back to stir the sauce and take another taste. I'm gonna tell Linda I lost the recipe and see if she gives me the same one. I smirk at my thought as Jax gathers his homework.

I dump the sauce over the meatballs and put them in the oven. I'll fry them at the end. Just like she does. They're the restaurant's best dish now that we fry them. I don't do much now that we have the managers, but I want our sauce to be the best. And I have the final say when it comes to the details.

I brace my hands on the small of my back and stretch. This little one better drop soon. It's getting hard to breathe.

"Alright, you hanging out with Mickey tonight?"

"Yup!" Jax answers, shoving the papers into his backpack.

"Just remember-" I start, but Jax cuts him off.

"I know, Mom! I'll call when I get there."

"Hey there, watch it." Dom scolds Jax even though he has a smile on his face. "You be respectful to your mother."

Jax sighs, "Sorry, Mom. Sorry, Dad. I just must be going through something." I have to turn and face the stove before I crack up laughing.

"Yeah, okay. Get outta here." Dom sends him away with a smile, and I finally turn around and lean against Dom.

His hands instantly go to my swollen belly, rubbing soothing circles. "How you feeling, doll?"

"Like I want this baby out." I do. I'm so done with being pregnant.

"Two more days." He kisses my belly. "Then finals will be done, and I won't have classes." I smile and let out an easy sigh.

"I know, Professor Valetti." I lean down and give him a slow kiss on his lips. "This little one is already a daddy's girl.

She's listening to you, not me."

The baby monitor goes off on the counter; Ethan's up. I check the clock and yup, it's been two hours. "That was a good nap." I yawn and pick it up and see our two-year-old rolling around and playing in his crib.

He laughs a low, deep chuckle against my lips. "Thank you, doll."

I pull back with a questioning look. "What'd you do that you're thanking me?"

He laughs and shakes his head. "Thank you for loving me."

My heart melts, and I mold my lips to his. He's so fucking sweet. "Always." I rub my hand along his stubble and give him a chaste kiss. "Love you."

"I love you too, doll."

ABOUT THE AUTHOR

Thank you so much for reading my romances. I'm just a stay at home Mom and an avid reader turned Author and I couldn't be happier.

I hope you love my books as much as I do!

More by Willow Winters
www.willowwinterswrites.com/books

Printed in the USA
CPSIA information can be obtained
at www.ICGtesting.com
JSHW022014191024
71938JS00006B/17